# PERFECTLY INCOMPATIBLE

## By Kathryn Anne Dubois

PERFECTLY INCOMPATIBLE
An Ellora's Cave Publication, January 2005

Ellora's Cave Publishing, Inc.
1337 Commerce Drive
Stow, Ohio 44224

ISBN #1-4199-5009-6

Perfectly Incompatible © 2004 Kathryn Anne Dubois
ISBN MS Reader (LIT) ISBN # 1-84360-908-8
Other available formats (no ISBNs are assigned):
Adobe (PDF), Rocketbook (RB), Mobipocket (PRC) & HTML

Cover art by *Syneca*

# Warning:

The following material contains graphic sexual content meant for mature readers. *Perfectly Imcompatible* has been rated *E-rotic* by a minimum of three independent reviewers.

Ellora's Cave Publishing offers three levels of Romantica™ reading entertainment: S (S-ensuous), E (E-rotic), and X (X-treme).

S-*ensuous* love scenes are explicit and leave nothing to the imagination.

E-*rotic* love scenes are explicit, leave nothing to the imagination, and are high in volume per the overall word count. In addition, some E-rated titles might contain fantasy material that some readers find objectionable, such as bondage, submission, same sex encounters, forced seductions, etc. E-rated titles are the most graphic titles we carry; it is common, for instance, for an author to use words such as "fucking", "cock", "pussy", etc., within their work of literature.

X-*treme* titles differ from E-rated titles only in plot premise and storyline execution. Unlike E-rated titles, stories designated with the letter X tend to contain controversial subject matter not for the faint of heart.

**Also by Kathryn Anne Dubois:**

A Man's Desire
Elemental Desires

# PERFECTLY INCOMPATIBLE

By Kathryn Anne Dubois

# Chapter One

"Go undercover as a married couple?" Libby responded, smoothing a damp palm along her cream linen skirt while her throat squeezed back the protest burning her lungs.

"That's right," Dr. Clark, the burly director of the FBI's vice team, said as he dumped a weighty packet in her lap and then into the hands of the Neanderthal seated next to her. The director eased back into his chair, tossing his pen on the tabletop. She would swear he was enjoying this.

But *she* wasn't laughing. Being partnered with a man she barely spoke to was no joke under the best of assignments. She respected Director Clark but silently questioned his sanity in making them a couple.

"Digest those materials, pack your bags, and notify friends and family. You start Friday."

Friday…the only bright spot in this mess. While she'd miss her father's fifty-eighth birthday dinner, she would *not* miss his endless praise of her three older brothers' expert running of the family business in which she was only permitted to own stock since she lacked the necessary equipment, a penis.

"Nailing the Brazilian cartel and their U.S. connection with this kind of scam satisfies my gut." He addressed Libby. "If you can tie names and dates and show the relationship between this clinic and drug lords, we can trace it to the mother lode." The director loosened his tie and then eyed her new partner/husband. "Michael, anything?"

The question had to be perfunctory, because in Libby's experience, Michael Mulcahy, prize investigator for the FBI, was known only to speak in grunts and nods. That he be expected to act like a normal husband--normal anything--on a marriage retreat/spa vacation with his wife was ludicrous.

She watched him peripherally. Without expression, he tilted back his chair and hooked an ankle over his knee. The man filled the room. It wasn't his size, although he *was* Penn State's former star quarterback. He just seemed to occupy more than his fair share of the air and space.

Between his lips rested the ever-present toothpick he chewed since he quit smoking--as if he needed anything to make him appear more sullen. The habitual rolling of the stick between his teeth made his face muscles flex, giving the hard line of his jaw an arrogant set that matched his disposition. She resisted the urge to fidget impatiently at the interminable wait for his reply to a simple question; she needed no reminder of how difficult he was.

Mulcahy dragged a hand over his dark thicket of hair and spoke. "Why us?"

Two words, barely audible, but there was no mistaking that rough "I just woke up, don't bother me" scowl to them.

"Because you're our best physical specimens." Clark leaned in. "Both of you. You'll fit in." His tone put to rest any thoughts of argument.

Libby kept quiet while she tugged at her hem, wishing she hadn't worn stockings that shimmered like silk. Out of habit, she tucked strands of her blonde hair behind one ear.

With a shrug, Mr. Personality lifted his six-foot-three frame, gave his boss a nod, and headed out without a glance at his future wife. She knew he still held her responsible for getting his partner transferred, but he could be a professional and let it go. Besides, it wasn't as though his partner had been given cafeteria duty; it had been a lateral reassignment.

She gave an invisible sigh of relief and then turned on the director she regarded as her mentor. "Richard, I don't know about this."

He scraped back his chair. "I do. You're professionals. Do what you're trained for."

"You see how he treats me—"

"Not on the job he won't. I know Michael better than anyone," he said evenly, trickling scotch over ice. He lifted a tumbler to her, but when she shook her head he rose and walked to the windows that overlooked Capitol Hill and peered out. "And because I know him," he said over his shoulder, "I'll bet he'll be in here as soon as you leave, saying the same thing. And I'll tell *him* the same thing. Whatever happened between you, I don't want to know." He turned to face her. "But solve it, because I'm no longer keeping you off assignments with each other."

Libby's eyes snapped to his. "Is that what he asked you to do?"

The director sighed. "Go pack and make sure you follow the inventory to the letter."

Because he hadn't denied it, Libby's uneasiness increased with the knowledge that Mulcahy had requested he not work with her. It was hard enough for a woman in this man's agency without the concealed hostility of the legendary Mulcahy to influence the rest of the team. While he never openly said a word against her, the very air between them bristled with tension, and because he was a "man's man," as her father would say, other agents followed his lead.

* * * * *

Libby dragged out the large leather suitcase from under her bed and plopped it onto her mattress. Although she was tempted to pack flannel pajamas, she couldn't take the chance that her role of "wife seeking to revive her marriage" be unconvincing. Besides, the resort was in Arizona and this was July.

She stuffed in the last of the lacy camisoles when she spied the engraved platinum roller pen that was her father's birthday present. She'd take it up Wednesday when she said goodbye. A quick goodbye, leaving no time for her mother's lectures about safe jobs, or feigned surprise from her brothers that she even *wanted* to work given the value of her stocks, along with subtle hints to cash in on those shares and along with it, her voting power.

She slammed her fourth suitcase closed.

Wouldn't they get a kick out of this assignment if they knew its nature. She'd be playing her mother--a dutiful wife. At least she had plenty of material to draw upon.

When the phone trilled, she picked up on the second ring.

"Nervous?" the familiar voice crooned.

Libby smiled into the receiver, picturing Morgan, one of the few female colleagues at the Bureau, whipping up brownies. She could hear her licking her fingers.

"Morgan, the assignment is absurd. I'm packing an outrageous assortment of underwear and nightgowns. Bureau orders."

"What'll *he* be wearing, is the question. Will it be large enough to cover all that male sinew, or not?" she teased.

"Cute. You obviously don't understand the ramifications."

"Oh, yes I do, and I'm jealous as hell."

"Right. You can have the assignment," Libby drawled.

This easy banter meant more to Libby than her friend could imagine. Growing up with a houseful of dominant males didn't prepare her for girlish camaraderie and had kept her isolated in high school. By college, her fierce academic competitiveness, in the misguided hope she'd be rewarded by her father, alienated her further. It wasn't until she'd graduated summa cum laude from Harvard, only to be denied any real position in the family business, that Libby realized what her father had been trying to tell her all along. He sent her to college to find a suitable husband. Not even her later graduation from the University of Pennsylvania's prestigious Wharton School with an MBA had changed his mind.

Morgan sighed. "I'll stick with financial fraud. But Lib, these situations will come up and unless you plan to transfer out—"

"No. That's probably what Mulcahy wants, and I won't give him the satisfaction. Besides, I don't think getting his partner transferred is all he holds against me. He's avoided me from the first day I joined the division, and today I found out he requested the director to keep me off his assignments."

"Okay," Morgan relented. "But I don't know how you'll do it."

"It's an advantage that we can't stand each other. We'll be living in close quarters, very close, pretending to work on a relationship while professionally adhering to strict Bureau policies against any physical involvement of agents. That'll be easy for us."

"Right. Agh. The brownies are burning. See you tomorrow."

\* \* \* \* \*

Libby took a steadying breath before entering the office of the Chief Coordinator of Logistics and gave herself a quick glance in the foyer mirror. She pulled at the sides of her hair, loosening a few stray tendrils at the crown to soften her French twist. She'd learned from Morgan that men expected their female colleagues to *look* feminine and *be* tough. Libby knew she came off cool and aloof. A few simple adaptations couldn't hurt. She wished someone had given her that advice earlier. Had she learned it, she might have fared better with the men and fit in with their easy banter.

She peered into her brown eyes and gave a cynical laugh. Apparently those experiments she studied in psychology where men perceived brown-eyed women as warmer than blue-eyed ones were flawed.

She opened the door to rich male laughter that stopped when they saw her.

"Libby…" Stephen Wilson smiled and motioned her to the chairs circling a cherry coffee table. Mulcahy was stretched out, his long legs crossed at the ankles. A bare nod was his only acknowledgement as she took the seat opposite him.

"I was just telling Michael about therapy sessions at the so-called spa."

"Starting without me?" she reprimanded and then could have kicked herself. They shouldn't have started, but she didn't have to be so flip, either.

"No," he assured her. "Michael got here a little early."

"Forgive me, Stephen." She sighed, removing her silk jacket and draping it over the back of her chair. "I'm a little edgy from all the last minute Bureau-dictated shopping."

"Sure, I understand. Let me get you some coffee."

When he leaped up and headed to the galley kitchen Libby wanted to scream, knowing she'd be alone with Stone Face and his glacial blue eyes that would freeze over when he looked at her. That experiment was right--blue eyes were cold...and unforgiving.

"Agent Mulcahy." She nodded, settling herself into the thick cushioned chair and casually crossing her legs.

He simply studied her, wordlessly, as though he had never seen her before, steel blue eyes raking down the complete length of her. If he was trying to look intimidating, he'd succeeded.

Stephen placed a steamy mug before her. "So, I was telling Michael that therapy sessions are part of the activities at this place."

"I read that, yes," Libby replied smoothly.

"And..." He chuckled lightly, but Libby could see he was uneasy. "I could give you fabricated problems but you already have issues between you. You'll actually appear authentic…as a couple."

Libby halted her cup midway to her lips and Mulcahy scowled.

"What I meant was…" Stephen chuckled amicably. "Some parameters will fit. You'll keep your real first names but your last name will be Meehan, to keep it Irish. With Michael's jet black hair and blue eyes he'd have to be, right 'Mick'?"

Mulcahy frowned.

"Good contrasts in those names," Stephen continued. "Libby's a wealthy New York debutante's name, which actually Libby is, and it'll work for her new identity, too. Michael will be from an Irish working class background of New York City cops and firefighters, which he is anyway. You, Libby, will remain cultured and aloof to Michael's usual surly and crude disposition and you should both be believable as a couple that needs help. With their marriage, that is."

Libby didn't know whether to laugh or snap at Stephen's inept assessment, so she simply took a lesson from Master Mulcahy and remained silent.

"And," Stephen continued, blissfully unaware of the tension in the room, "since you are both exercise nuts, you'll have no problem with the spa part."

He looked from one to the other, pleased, as though he was sending his twins off to camp for the summer.

The leather billfold he handed them contained all the last minute fabricated identification and personalized paraphernalia they would need to put the finishing touches on their identities.

"Look at this one." Stephen held up a gold locket in the shape of a claddagh, with the fingers of the entwined hands beautifully etched to catch light. "Michael gave it to you for your fifth anniversary. Even had it inscribed. Nice touch, huh?"

Stephen grinned.

The air was thick and still.

Libby couldn't help but smile when Stephen continued to look at her expectantly, his eyes huge behind his thick-rimmed glasses. "It's lovely," she assured him. "Very believable, all of it."

He seemed touched by her confidence, and she found it endearing. He hardly needed her approval. He might be nerdy at times, but he was the youngest handwriting and documentation expert in the country.

Blue Eyes was watching her again, his expression impassive.

\* \* \* \* \*

The wait for the cab that would take them to the resort was suffocating, but not due to record temperatures of 120 degrees. The chill alone coming from Mulcahy should have kept her plenty cool. This was never going to work, she thought.

"Look." She turned, tilting her five-foot-eight frame to face him squarely. Then she groaned inwardly, thankful that her large tortoise shell sunglasses hid her expression. His eyes matched the blue cloudless sky behind him. And his lashes were ridiculously thick. Enough to make her forget he was a jerk--almost. She made herself concentrate on the thin scar that ran along his brow.

He lifted it now in question while he painstakingly reached into his breast pocket for his mirrored glasses, never breaking her gaze. The icy blues disappeared behind the mirrors.

She spoke to her reflection.

"Look, you can dispense with making a point of not speaking to me. It must take an enormous amount of energy and considerable forethought to accomplish and it would be wiser to save your energy for this assignment."

His lips parted, barely.

She waited.

Nothing discernible followed.

She shifted her weight and fought the compulsion to tuck her hair behind one ear. The blistering heat scorched her skin but she would not fidget and give him the impression she was anxious, though she was.

"We're adults, doing a job," she sniffed. "And it hardly looks natural for us to literally say nothing to each other."

No response, unless she could count the action of his propping the damned toothpick between his teeth and rolling it. A muscle jumped over the dark shadow of his jaw.

"We don't have to confess any deep dark secrets." She tried to put an easy spin on it, but she could feel the light pulse at the base of her neck quickening. "A few civil words will do."

Oppressive silence. She might as well be talking to herself. She was. Her reflection paid close attention.

"You can speak now," she drawled, unable to tolerate his rudeness a moment longer. Where was that skycap with their cab? Her eyes searched for the attendant.

"Okay." The quiet deep baritone was distinctly his. A miracle.

She glanced at him uncertainly. He snapped the toothpick off in his teeth. She resumed her scanning of the crowd and stifled a sigh. One word. It was a start.

\* \* \* \* \*

The lobby of polished stone floors and pastel furniture was brightened with couples looking delighted to be on their quest for a new and improved marriage.

The glass elevator, centered in the palm covered reception area, allowed Libby a quick view of the resort's layout as it slid upward. Tiered indoor balconies surrounded the perimeter of the first three floors, and through the glassed front she saw a large golf course to the east and several pools at its south end. She could only imagine how much it cost to keep those lush greens watered in this veritable desert, miles from nowhere.

A dome-shaped annexed building that caught her eye surprised her since she hadn't remembered it from the preliminary report.

She glanced at Mulcahy. He was looking up at where the elevator walls met the ceiling, his usually expressionless face taut with tension. She followed the direction of his gaze and saw the oil paintings that lined the entire perimeter. Her mouth dropped.

The paintings depicted more variations of coitus than Libby knew even existed. She flushed at the sight of a full-figured Rubenesque-like model on hands and knees licking the purpled head of her partner's penis. His neck was thrown back in abandon, his fists buried in her long red hair, and droplets of his semen glistened on her lips. Libby swallowed.

Out of the corner of her eye she watched Mulcahy tip his head to one side as he studied another painting, that of a single woman with three men. Libby felt her skin heat as she tried to imagine if what they were doing was even possible.

The art was early 18th Century. The men were all fully dressed in fine velvet frocks while the woman wore only an ivory chemise, her rouged nipples poking above the lace trim. She was propped on all fours, impaled by the man beneath her, with another kneeling beside her, impaling her mouth. The third man was poised behind her, his erection in hand, directing it between her bared buttocks. He looked abnormally large, or at least in her limited experience it seemed so. Libby swallowed.

Libby felt Mulcahy's eyes on her. She eyed him coolly. "Interesting choice of paintings for an elevator. Perhaps they plan regular emergency stops to give couples time to revive their sex life." Although she was dying inside, she'd be damned if she let him know.

She would have thought him cool and collected if she only observed his facial expression but she hadn't moved up the ranks of the FBI as fast as she did by missing subtle clues. Mulcahy's eyes were smoldering. The fire that it started in her went straight to her groin, instantly wetting her panties. She dropped her glance. A mistake. A full erection pressed against his fly.

She stifled a groan, relieved when the elevator slid open for them to exit.

She had barely cooled down when they reached their room. Francisco, their personal attendant, greeted them. "Mr. and Mrs. Meehan, your schedules are posted. Dinner is at seven o'clock in the Crescent Ballroom, semi-formal for the first evening." His white teeth flashed against a healthy tan. "If there is any way I can serve you before then, ring the front desk and request me personally. Our job is to keep your time here stress free." He beamed, his friendly enthusiasm so charming that she had to remind herself he could be their number one smuggler.

"Thank you, Francisco."

Mr. Sociability barely nodded. They must look like one couple in serious trouble. It was ironic that they looked quite adorable. Mulcahy's biceps were twice the width of her waist. Like Barbie and Ken. Libby grimaced. Except that Barbie's breasts were bigger than hers.

When Francisco set down the bags, Mulcahy fisted some bills into his hand. The young man smiled broadly and scurried out.

As soon as the door closed, the effect of the air conditioner hit, and her nipples tightened into pebbles beneath her silky sundress. "It must be sixty degrees in here. Mind if I turn up the temperature?" She glanced at him, expecting a grunt, but he took off his glasses and walked slowly toward her, his eyes dropping to her breasts.

A light shiver slid over her. He kept coming.

She saw what he planned on doing, it was clear in his eyes, but the thought was so absurd that her brain short-circuited and went numb. Even as he reached out with one large hand and caught her easily by the waist, she didn't believe it. It was someone else he was encircling in his arms and drawing in close, hip to hip.

She stared at his lips as they descended. It was as though she was watching a film set in slow motion. This wasn't her and it wasn't his mouth, relaxed and parted, his eyes heavy-lidded.

He pressed his mouth against hers and brushed lightly, his manner unhurried, as though this was natural for them. His arms felt like tree trunks encircling her. The warm taste of him sent blood flooding back to her brain and then it pumped everywhere...her head, her throat, her breasts...Lord. He smelled completely male—a touch of soap and leather. She felt his erection swelling against her belly.

He licked her bottom lip.

"Mulcha—"

"Jesus, Libby." He nipped at her mouth. "Don't forget our names, for Chrissake," he murmured against her lips.

One hand stroked her bare back and the feel of his fingertips, warm on her skin, set her pulse racing.

"Can you see any obvious bugs?" he whispered, turning his head to one side and then the other as he brushed back and forth along her lip, his breath warm against her mouth, while his massive frame surrounded her, drawing her up against rock-hard thighs.

He cupped her bottom and squeezed.

"No." She pushed against the granite wall of his chest. "And there are other ways to find out." She bit down on his tongue. He jumped back, pressing the back of his hand to his mouth.

He smiled, his gleam wicked. "You want it rough, baby? Okay, I like that game too."

Her eyes widened in horror when he came at her fast and scooped her up in his arms. "We're taking a shower."

She was hallucinating. Mr. Withdrawn Taciturn had turned into a maniac. In her struggle with him, her slip of a sundress hiked up around her waist, and he was feasting his eyes on the scrap of lace from Victoria's Secret that passed for panties. She snatched at the hem but not in time to prevent him from clamping his mouth onto her thigh.

She choked on a gasp.

Once in the bathroom, he dropped her onto her feet. "Strip off that dress, darlin'." The blue of his eyes glittered with tension as he kicked the door closed.

She stood, gaping and clutching her skirt, while her mind raced. When he advanced on her, she pivoted, ready with a groin punt, but he swept by and flung open the glass shower door. He turned on the pulsating jets of the massager.

"That's good, baby, peel it off real slow," he said to the ceramic tiled wall as he ducked his head, examining the levers and then kneeling down to run his fingers along the door frame.

He rose and dragged off his loafers before pulling his shirt over his head and dropping it onto the floor.

He was a study in masculinity, all hard planes and muscle under smooth golden skin. Her eyes riveted on the dark dusting of hair along his chest.

His head crooked, he gave an impatient frown and pointed to her sandals. He waited, hands on hips, with his eyes surveying the room and then finally settling on the overhead light. When he reached to feel around the crystal rim, his pants dropped low on his hips. Her eyes helplessly traced the dark line of hair that narrowed and disappeared under his belt.

She drew in a calming breath and then admonished herself to get with the program before she made a complete fool of herself. At least anyone listening couldn't mistake *her* for a top notch FBI agent.

After she kicked off her sandals, she joined him in the shower, thankful it was designed to fit two.

Giving the spray a hard shove, he angled it at the wall and then leaned against the glass and folded his arms.

Steam floated between them and a light mist settled on their clothes and skin. The moisture plastered her dress to her nipples. His gaze dropped and lingered before returning to her face. His eyelashes glistened with water.

She glanced around efficiently. "I don't think we have to worry about listening devices in here, and I doubt they'd bother with cameras in the bathroom."

"Uh huh…" He swiped a hand through his hair.

"I'll play the cleanliness obsessed wife and have us scour the place for germs."

"Good idea."

"But lets start with this bathroom anyway, just to be sure."

"Right."

* * * * *

Greenwood Country Manor, covering two hundred acres of rich blooming desert, had a guest capacity of one thousand. Sessions ran regularly all year.

On the surface nothing looked amiss. For two hours Libby and Michael discreetly combed the area together, but the blistering heat kept them and most of the guests near the pools or indoors. The golf course was deserted, as were the walking paths. Even the white flagstone between buildings was so hot that the soles of their feet burned through their shoes.

The air was as dry as a sauna but very breezy.

"It feels like a dozen blow-dryers are aimed at my face," Libby said as they headed back to their suite to change for dinner.

"Yeah."

"What do you make of the dome? I'd like to know what 'special sessions' are keeping it closed."

"Me, too."

When she suggested Michael slip into the main office later that evening and see what he could lift, he agreed. Something had to turn up that would give them information about covert activities for which this place served as a cover.

As soon as they entered their suite, they checked trip points for indicators of intruders. Everything was clean.

Michael showered first. Libby said she needed time to set up. He was curious about what that meant. By the time he finished dressing, she reappeared with an iron, more hangers and extra towels of various sizes. He couldn't imagine what such a delicately boned woman would need with so many towels. A host of bottles and accoutrements was strewn along the surface of the dressing table and it irritated him that he was interested in seeing what she planned to do with them.

When he checked his watch, he saw that he had a half hour until dinner, so he propped the oversized lace pillows on the king-sized bed, stretched out his legs and hit the remote. Yankees versus Red Socks. Four to zip, Red Socks. He frowned. They still had a chance.

He muted the TV. Its wide screen recessed into an oak cabinet it shared with a five-changer CD system. Depressing the button activated the first program in the system and Eric Clapton's croon filled the air. He glanced around. Flowered wallpaper and frosted lamps gave the room the kind of old-fashioned look that women liked. Fresh orchids, stuck in one of those chipped looking vases, took up most of one small table in the sitting area. They must have come while he was showering. He'd remember to ask Libby.

*Libby.*

He listened to the shower running and dragged his hands down his face. His tension returned.

When Clark first dumped this assignment on him, he was stunned. He tried to talk him out of it. Richard knew he couldn't work with her and had promised to keep them apart, but now the director had changed his mind and wouldn't budge. Michael had no choice but to find a way to make it work to his advantage, and finally he had. He would settle this thing with her. He would not repeat his brothers' mistakes. Besides, it was unfair to Maggie to keep putting her off.

One thing he would *not* do was get sidetracked anymore by Libby Crowne Vandermark. Christ...even her name was a nightmare. At thirty-six, he needed someone like Maggie O'Doole, who'd gladly quit her job to raise their kids and maybe even plant some geraniums by the white picket fence. With his demanding profession, he could settle for no less.

Now that he was here with Libby and would be in this room day after day—

and night—he would face down this lust thing and be done with it.

The TV flashed. He looked up to see Jeter hit a triple, down the line. It was about time. Yankees had two outs and Bernie was up. "Come on, Bernie, just get on base," Michael murmured.

If she weren't such a tangle of contrasts he doubted he'd be attracted to her. But he'd seen her in action during interrogations. Like a newly graduated coed she'd appeal to the suspect's patience while flashing some leg. Flustered, they'd spill their guts and then she'd go for the jugular.

Those milk chocolate eyes would harden and even when the suspects leaped across the table her thick lashes never blinked. Some of the men easily doubled her in weight.

He ran a finger under his neck collar.

How could such light hair go with those dark brows and lashes? And while she looked like an ice figurine with that pale skin and slight frame, she was tall for a woman and no fragile doll. She was…irregular. Nothing about her really fit.

His fingers worked the back of his neck.

Playing the loving husband, seeking to repair his marriage, gave him the perfect opportunity to seduce her and finally rid himself of his relentless desire for her.

He bolted upright and glared at the TV. Strike three. Top of the ninth. "For Chrissake. Swing at it, Bernie."

Michael bit down on the toothpick.

Clark had been amazed by Michael's change of perspective on this assignment. Maybe he'd get a promotion when it was over. And he would come to some decision about Maggie O'Doole. Even his brother had been bugging him about it.

This thing with Libby was just physical, nothing to get tied up over. He reached instinctively to feel the tender end of his tongue. One problem. Libby was not going to be easy to seduce.

The bathroom door swung open, and she emerged in a fresh terry robe, head bent and hair tousled as she riffled her fingers through the pale strands. She didn't see him until she sat at the ornate dressing mirror and caught his reflection.

"Oh..." She turned casually. "I thought you'd gone downstairs."

He focused on the TV. "If I keep leaving every time you change it'll look suspicious."

She shrugged lightly. "You're probably right." Picking up a small bottle, she shook it and never glanced at him again while he feigned interest in the game.

When she got to her lips, it was hard not to watch her. The lipstick's shade of color, like rich mahogany wood, slid that wet look over her lips. Another contrast. For while she had a regal manner about her in the way she would lift the slim tip of her nose or arch a brow in disapproval, her lips were made for sex. Full and soft, dark red even without lipstick.

Their eyes met in the mirror, hers questioning.

"Ready yet?" he asked. The toothpick broke off in his mouth.

"In a minute," she responded.

Back into the bathroom, a few minutes of listening to the blow dryer, and she was out again, walking to the closet in a tiny black shift of a dress that barely covered her nipples, erect now and thrusting against the silky cloth. After a full day of her wearing dresses without a bra beneath, he could see that her breasts were small and high, beautifully shaped.

As she slipped into a pair of satiny black heels with ankle straps, he put on his own dress loafers and jacket, without giving her another glance. He didn't trust himself not to grab her up and take a bite out of her.

# Chapter Two

Libby studied their dinner companions, looking for a common thread, something to give her a clue and point them toward the true operations of this place and its source of revenue. The doctor and his wife were her parents' age and from Los Angeles. The rich bronze of her skin bespoke of a Hispanic heritage while he resembled a well-aged surfer, with his graying, neatly trimmed beard and small ponytail.

Colleen and Sean McDermott, barely in their twenties, were from Philadelphia and ran their own industrial cleaning business. She was an adorable petite redhead and he looked like a smaller, less dramatic version of Mulcahy. Terrell and Belinda, an exceptionally attractive African-American couple about her own age of twenty-eight from the Chicago suburbs, laughed easily while she recited the horrors of teaching Middle School. He was a computer scientist.

The doctor was looking at Mulcahy and Sean with that vague look people who know nothing about sports get when confronted with jocks. Mulcahy seemed not to notice and nodded when Sean starting ribbing the doctor about Shaq—whoever that was—not winning the scoring title a few years back. Sean then gloated about Allen Iverson taking the title from this Shaq. Mulcahy smiled, obviously enjoying the conversation.

Colleen leaned over and whispered, "Your husband's very handsome."

The comment took Libby by surprise, because she'd been struggling to avoid thinking about Michael at all. His presence was already too strong and pervasive within the confines of their small suite. She glanced his way. He and Sean were waving their arms animatedly, imitating what looked like slam-dunks, if she recognized it right from watching her brothers. She thought she had never seen him so enthusiastic, but then she recalled hearing his deep laughter with Stephen before their meeting.

"Of course he's handsome," Libby teased. "He could pass for your husband's older brother."

The young woman smiled.

Mulcahy glanced up to see her looking at him. He flashed her a small smile that caught her unaware, his eyes lingering a bit. She drew in a shaky breath and tamped out the flicker of heat that ignited in the pit of her belly. He played his part well, she ruefully admitted, and then chided herself to get back to work.

Scanning the room, her only conclusion was that this was a dead end; no common thread, unless the overall attractiveness of the group counted.

A moment later, Mulcahy grabbed her hand and tugged her to the dance floor. He drew her close, settling his leg between hers and his lips into her hair. The warmth of his body mingling with hers drew an uneasy sigh from her lips.

"Anything?" he murmured into her ear, his warm breath caressing her neck. She felt ridiculously small in his arms, not a comfortable feeling for an agent. Good thing they were on the same side.

"Not so far," she responded, businesslike, which wasn't easy since he was now nibbling on the delicate skin of the back of her earlobe. A light tingle ran down her spine and her body began to heat.

"Libby?" He shifted and slid his hand down to the small of her back, applying a pressure so subtle she wasn't sure if she imagined it.

And she hoped she only imagined the firm presence of something pressing against her lower belly. He shifted again and this time it was not her imagination. She panicked, unsure of how to handle this. What if it was just his belt buckle?

He whispered in her ear. "I've got to get into that office before the evening ends. It'll be less conspicuous than if I roam around in the dark while everyone else is asleep." Her heart pounded in her chest. A subtle movement had his hand dipping lower, resting at the curve where her back met her bottom. "I'll start by dusting for prints."

"Okay," she breathed, lulled by his clean male scent and the deliberate brush of his rough shadow along her chin. She had prepared herself for all manner of horrors connected with this ordeal with him: blatant hostility, cool disregard, and constant antagonism. But she had not prepared herself for this. The feel of his body shifting against hers; the sheer warmth was like a soothing massage sucking her under and making her weak.

"Make an excuse. I'll need about fifteen minutes," he murmured, running his tongue down her throat. The wet warmth of it sent her pulse skyrocketing. In an instinctive gesture, she pressed her breasts against his chest. He drew her over to a dim corner.

"Libby?" His voice was hoarse as he dipped to press his mouth against hers, sliding his tongue restlessly along her bottom lip. "I leave at exactly nine."

She gasped silently as he pressed his hips to hers, flattening her to the wall. She looked up into the startling blue of his eyes. When had they stopped dancing? Now she knew what was pressing against her and it was no belt buckle. The hard ridge of his erection was impossible to ignore. His eyes were feverish. Her blood fired, deep and low.

"Mulcahy," she said, her tone airy. "You really don't have to work this hard."

"You know about being married?" He cocked his head.

"Not personally, but—"

"My parents were all over each other."

"That's precious. But unless you brought your gun, I'm wondering what's pressing against me."

He grunted. "The little guy has a life of his own."

"*Little* guy?" She gave him a firm push.

"Uh…Libby. Since I don't have my jacket, you're going to have to give me a minute. I can't walk back to the table like this."

Her heart pounded at the sound of the arousal threading his voice.

She squirmed beneath him.

He clutched her hips. "Don't do that." He closed his eyes and breathed through his nostrils.

Her skin flushed at the feel of him through his thin linen pants. She barely resisted the urge to slide herself against him, closing her mind instead against the erotic image.

"You've got to stay still, Libby."

"*I'm* not moving." She lifted a brow. "You are."

He groaned. "Jesus."

"Have you been celibate for the past year or something?"

He groaned again.

He lifted himself off her but clutched her waist. "Just wait here so I look like I have a reason for facing the wall. Pretend we're talking."

She was thankful for the break in contact, but the weight of his hands resting on her hips did nothing to relieve her tension. The heat from their bodies mixed and he tightened his hands reflexively as he took cleansing breaths. Her dress was so light, she felt like he was touching her bare skin. He slid his hands quickly down her hips.

Before she could protest, he grabbed her hand and led her away. What had just happened?

Then she reminded herself he was just doing a job.

\* \* \* \* \*

It was eleven o'clock by the time they finished dinner. Michael laid the fax machine out flat on the coffee table in their suite and dialed Clark while he watched Libby disappear in and out of the bathroom. He couldn't figure out if she was anxious or just disorganized. He decided it was the latter because Libby was unflappable.

He wondered what *would* get a rise out of her. Apparently it took more than his obvious arousal with her at dinner. His rock-hard cock only slightly annoyed her and never interrupted her flawless interrogation later of the guests as she insinuated herself into their confidence. If the Bureau needed allies down the road she had them well primed, and with her clever questioning, if something was suspicious, she'd uncover it.

She swept out again, her heels and stockings discarded, but with her bare slip of a dress still intact. As she rifled through her drawer again, he realized she was grabbing out nightgowns and figured she was trying to select one for tonight. But then he dismissed the thought. If Libby was anything, it was cool. It would take a lot more than his rampant lust to break through the glaze of ice surrounding her.

And he wanted to…and wondered again what it would take. To just crack the glaze a bit. He determined to find out tonight, because while formerly he had thought with more contact it would get easier, this raging lust was now worse than ever.

"Come here, Libby," he called to her as he tried the number again when the first connection didn't take. "I'll unzip your dress." He feigned distraction with the machine while watching her every move.

She glanced up. "I'm fine." She tossed the comment over her shoulder and disappeared into the bathroom for the third time.

The screen flashed "message received." He snapped the case shut and stowed it under the bed.

Although the bed was turned down, he dumped himself atop the covers in an effort to keep her from snuggling under too soon. He was looking forward to seeing her sprawled out beside him.

When she came out again, she still wore that damned dress. This time, she wouldn't get away.

"For Chrissake, Libby. Let me get that dress for you. How'd you get into that thing, anyway?"

"Oh." She glanced down as though just discovering that she hadn't changed. Knowing females had a thing about bathrooms, he wondered if she was doing other things behind that door. He would enjoy imagining *exactly* what.

She perched herself on the edge of the bed.

"Thanks," she said lightly.

He allowed his fingertips to trail along her skin as the zipper separated. "You might have gotten sunburned with that dress you had on earlier." He ran the palm of his hand down the length of her bare back. She was like silk. A delicate scent kissed the air.

"I'm fine." She moved to rise.

"Wait." The zipper slipped lower, just enough to reveal black lace panties. This was self-torture. "Your skin feels hot." He smoothed his hand along her spine.

If she was uncomfortable, she gave no indication, making the temptation to slip his fingers under the thin strip of elastic separating his palm from the smooth skin of her bottom almost impossible to resist. But that was pressing his luck.

"You want me to put something on it?"

She stood and turned to him, holding up the front of her dress. With no bra underneath, all it would take was a little tug. Her expression was indiscernible.

"Something to take the heat out," he explained.

He thought maybe he had chinked the ice with this last stunt because she looked poised on the edge of something. Their eyes met; hers pensive, curious, while he could feel his own smoldering.

She studied him quietly.

"No." She flicked the bottom of her hair over her shoulder and turned with the ease of a woman sure of herself. "It's not bothering me."

His fingers sizzled from the feel of her and the erection he was controlling grew another inch as she walked away, the silky back of her dress barely concealing her lace covered backside.

He raked a tortured hand through his hair and growled.

He decided to get under the covers.

She finally emerged in an ivory nightshirt that barely cleared the tops of her thighs, calling attention to her long legs and teasing his brain into guessing whether she wore panties or not. Of course, she would wear them. Probably a matching silk pair with lacy elastic that he could hook his fingers around and slide off. Although the silk shirt amply covered her, the smooth fabric clung to every sensuous curve. Her erect nipples puckered the cloth into delectable peaks.

He wanted her. The thought filled him...with both mental yearning and a physical ache. And nagged at him. Because there was no way she'd succumb to him this soon—if ever. And he didn't know how he would survive this.

"Can *I* get in there now?" he asked, indicating the bathroom and giving her a half grin.

She appeared surprised by his relaxed tone, but he wasn't sure. She was almost impossible to read.

When he returned from the bathroom, he flipped through the science magazine he'd bought in the gift shop and tried not to look as she brushed her hair with idle strokes.

"Mulcahy, if you'd feel more comfortable, we could put a row of pillows between us."

"Me?" He gave an amused frown as she approached the bed, limbs of satin gliding beneath silk. His palms itched to slide his hands up her thighs as she lifted the bed covers and perched on the edge.

"I guess it is a big bed," she said.

"Call me Michael."

She hesitated a fraction before flattening her palms against her hem and swinging her legs up onto the bed. His tension took another leap. Damn, he'd like to know what she wore under there.

"You might slip up when we're outside this room," he explained.

"Yes, you're right," she said, picking up a paperback by the lamp. *Total Control* by David something. *Some title.*

"Self-help book?" He glanced at her lap.

"Actually, it's a novel…about an FBI investigation."

"Ah…" *Work. Same thing.*

He was crazy to think he could do this. She was too smart and not interested in anything so sordid as sweaty sex with a man with whom she was barely on speaking terms.

"Um…Michael."

It gave him a jolt to hear his name from those lips. He wasn't surprised that when he looked at her he was unable to resist studying them.

Whatever she intended to say she didn't, apparently having changed her mind, for she pretended concern over the lights instead. When she started to get out of bed, he stopped her with a restraining hand on her bare arm, allowing his touch to linger.

"I'll get them. I've got to set the door anyway."

He set a string by the threshold and then hit the overhead lights. They would know if anyone even cracked the door an inch.

When he got back into bed, he grabbed the remote, intending to find some baseball, tennis, he'd even settle for golf, but what he found was even better. The TV had to be rigged. Every channel was set to an adult movie.

Libby gasped beside him.

He smiled to himself. A redhead with tits the size of watermelons was bending forward, stripping panties down her thighs in a slow seductive tease for three fully clothed guys who sat in easy chairs watching her.

"Change the channel," Libby snapped.

He flipped through the remote. "It won't make any difference," he chuckled. "They're all..." His words dropped to a whisper. "Aw, Jesus." His cock pounded to life.

A tall blonde actress, almost as pretty as Libby, was pinned against a wall by a dark, tall, muscular type who had his hand curled into the front of her sundress. He yanked, baring her small breasts. His large hands completely covered them.

"Michael, turn off the TV."

"Just a minute." The guy was pinching the blonde's nipples.

Libby grabbed for the remote but he held it away from her.

"Shit." The guy pushed the actress's dress up to her waist and dipped his hand into her panties. Michael's erection tented the sheets.

Libby climbed over top of him, reaching for the remote, her backside poised right above his groin. Without thinking he palmed her bottom.

She twisted and slapped at his hand just as the actress began moaning.

"What are you doing, you lunatic?"

Michael groaned. "Exactly what this place expects us to do when they planned this."

She knelt beside him. "Not *us*. Married couples. Have you forgotten why we're here?"

"Yeah." He swallowed, his eyes settling on her nipples, hard points now against her silky top. "It's not hard to do."

"Well, you better *not* forget or we'll blow this assignment." She scurried down underneath the covers, escaping his lecherous gaze.

He ran a hand down his face. *Christ.* If things got any worse, he'd never make it. *They got worse.* When he looked up, the guy had his dick out and was aiming it at the blonde's shaved pussy. He was separating her glistening slit with his fingers, and with one good shove he fucked her. Michael groaned.

When he glanced down at Libby she had the covers pulled up to her ears and she was fuming. "Aw, come on.

It wasn't that bad." He gave her a teasing grin. She glared at him. Even so, what he wouldn't *give* to settle his face between Libby's thighs and taste her.

Reluctantly, he killed the TV and returned to his *Scientific American*. He found the article about solar energy by Wienberg and Williams and tried to finish it, but he couldn't concentrate. He breathed deep and concentrated instead on relaxing so his erection would subside.

If anyone told him he'd be sitting next to Libby in a king-sized bed reading a magazine, he'd have bet any amount of money against it. In the last six months he'd tried *not* to think about Libby in his bed, and a magazine never entered the fantasy. The scene had the quality of a bizarre parody.

He stole a glimpse. Her face was clean of makeup but no less startling, only younger looking and fresher. She had a glow to her cheeks and nose. He dropped his gaze. Her nipples were erect again. He could even see the tiny bumps around the tips.

"I'm going to turn down the air conditioner," he said casually.

"Fine." Obviously still irritated with him, she didn't even spare him a glance.

He threw the indicator up and then thought a minute before he pushed it up to ninety-eight and smiled to himself.

When he returned to bed she had turned off her light and was burrowed under the sheets.

He clicked off his own lamp. It wasn't going to be easy falling asleep while he could smell the clean scent of her just inches away.

# Chapter Three

The soft moaning filtered through Michael's sleepy haze and woke him with a start. He glanced at the clock. Three a.m. Libby's hair lay in a tangle across the pillow, and the covers and sheets were in a heap at the foot of the bed. Sprawled out on her stomach with one leg bent to her chest, her nightshirt had hiked up to her waist and he was looking at the delicious sight of her silken-covered backside, the soft rounded curves a kiss away. For a slim woman she was well filled out.

He was hard before he could complete the thought, which further drew him to implement the plan he'd formed before he finally fell asleep last night. He had already convinced himself that it made sense on some scientific level, which wasn't difficult. Now he had to convince her.

She tossed restlessly and turned, facing him, her lips morning-soft and relaxed in sleep. Innocent. He wanted to taste her again but that wasn't plausible. The fine motor precision of a kiss would fall under suspicion. He'd stick with his original plan.

He snuggled up close, wrapping his leg around hers and pressing his hips against the soft swell of her bottom. The silk of her panties felt surprisingly cool against the slippery fabric of his own silk boxers. The sliding of fabric stimulated him further and he groaned audibly and tucked her head under his chin. She fit perfectly within the angles of his body, her soft curves filling each space.

She smelled delicious. The light sheen of sweat from the heat moistened her skin and a fragrance of soap and shampoo—a honey scent—mixed with her expensive perfume. He breathed in a delicious breath.

She shifted restlessly in response to her body absorbing his heat.

He allowed himself the innocent pleasure of resting his hand on seldom-touched skin at the base of her spine.

She moaned softly, awakening.

He closed his eyes and waited.

"Michael…" She squirmed and pushed up with her bottom. He growled deep in his chest. If that was all he got it'd be worth it.

She repeated his name, sounding slightly panicked. "Wake up."

He groaned and pulled her tighter against him, pressing wickedly into her bottom.

"Oh my God," she breathed.

He'd cracked the glaze.

When she jerked her head up he heard a distinctive pop in his chin. *So much for the seductive sliding of their bodies as he awakened by microseconds.*

He murmured a sleepy sound. Her own response erupted into a quick jab to his gut.

With a reluctant sigh, he opened his eyes and met her incensed orbs, just inches away. Her eyes widened incredulously. "What are you doing?"

He propped himself up on one elbow with a lazy effort and gave a dazed scan of the room while she scurried onto her knees, tugging her nightshirt over her legs. She flicked on the lamp. They were both perched precariously on the edge of one eighth of the king-sized bed—her side.

She fanned herself. "Why is it so hot in here?" She slipped off the bed and checked the thermostat. With a tap of her finger, the fan rumbled.

He feigned a slumbering ignorance. "What time is it?" He fumbled for the clock. "Did you hear something? Check the string."

She gave an exasperated sigh, but to his delight, turned and bent to check the trap anyway. He peered under the hem of her nightshirt at the swell of her lacy bottom.

"It's fine," she reported, straightening and giving a tug at her hem. He could tell she was unsure as her eyes swept over him and then glanced away. Her hair was in disarray and her lips looked full and soft from sleep.

He leaned back into the pillows and folded his arms, posturing some frustration of his own. "What is it, Libby?"

"Look at where you are," she said with annoyance, regarding the empty three quarters of his side of the bed.

"Oh..." He gave a careless shrug and let his eyes melt over her. "Well, it's only natural." He was hoping his twelve-year subscription to *Scientific American* and *Omni Magazine* would pay off.

She blinked.

"It's bound to happen," he explained.

Her eyes narrowed and then brightened to a bronze sheen, reflecting the light from the bedside lamp. "What?"

He eased off the mattress and with a casual wave of his hand indicated the bed. "This..." With his back to her, he walked to the windows and drew aside the curtain. "Looks quiet."

"What is?"

"The activity," he replied.

"What is *natural*?" she persisted coolly, despite the enticing blush that spread along the tops of her breasts.

"That we would be attracted to each other."

She gave him a bored stare. "Right," she drawled. "We don't even like each other." With a relaxed step, she walked casually over to the small bar.

He'd never known a woman so cool under pressure. She dropped cubes into a tall frosted glass.

"Yeah." He shrugged noncommittally, letting the curtain drop and following her to the bar. He had her convinced his actions were involuntary. Now for part B of his plan. "The trouble is our bodies don't know it, it's just instinct." He drew up close, allowing the coarse hair on his thigh to brush against the silken skin on hers while he clinked ice into a tumbler.

She gave an incredulous chuckle. "Hardly." She smiled indulgently and then shook her head in amusement, apparently delighted by his little theory.

She needed a demonstration.

He dragged her against him and covered her mouth with his, claiming her with his tongue the way he wanted to with his body. Her nipples tightened against his chest. When she released a strangled cry, he set her from him and dropped an insolent gaze to her breasts. "See?"

Her hand came slamming up to his face, which he caught in one quick motion, encircling her tiny wrist. His first reaction was surprise at such a womanly response.

"A *slap*, Libby?"

No sooner had he uttered the words before she dropkicked a cut to his groin. He hunched over, pain searing through him.

"Oh my God," she gasped.

The air left his lungs in a whoosh. Somewhere in the recesses of his brain he wondered if he lived.

She dropped beside him. "Michael, are you all right?"

He was curled so tightly he rolled onto his head. An animal groan echoed from his stomach.

"I'm sorry, Michael. I just...reacted. Can you get up?"

"Like I said," he croaked. "Some things are just instinct."

"Let me help you—"

"No." He held up a hand. "I'll do it myself." He pulled himself over to the bed.

"Can I get you some ice?" She hovered over him.

"Ice?" He looked at her blankly. "Libby. Just give me a minute to breathe." He wound himself into a ball and sucked in slow drafts of air. "This takes care of *my* instinctual reactions for awhile."

Even his breathing came out in long groans.

* * * * *

The psychologist's office was airy, with bright watercolors between the large windows. Libby made a mental note of the graduation dates on the framed certificates: Berkley '90 and Stanford in '93. She would be about Michael's age.

"Now that we've concluded the preliminary intake, let's move to this cozy area overlooking the golf course, shall we?"

Since the doctor was walking toward the circle of easy chairs as she spoke, it was hardly a question she was asking. Libby glanced at Michael just as his eye caught hers in a commiserating glance that she found oddly comforting.

"So, Libby," Dr. Adler addressed her. "May I call you Libby?" Since she already had, any objection Libby voiced would be recorded as "resistant to counseling." She had been through enough of these to know. Libby barely smiled.

"Good." Of course the doctor took it as affirmative.

Libby couldn't wait to see how Michael cooperated in this first session.

Dr. Adler settled her petite figure into the chair and crossed her legs decorously. Her fitted shirt rode up a titch. Soft waves of burgundy hair framed large green eyes and little bow lips. She was adorable. Libby glanced at Michael. Michael looked on in rapt attention.

"I see you're a marketing executive, Libby. Do you enjoy your work?"

The irony of the question. If it was her profession, she'd love it. But vice-president of marketing for Vandermark & Sons Department Store Chains went to her second oldest brother, although he would have preferred finance.

"Yes, I've worked hard to get where I am, and I take my profession seriously."

"I see," Dr. Adler replied insightfully. "Do I detect some defensiveness, Libby?"

*Here we go.* Let's analyze everything to death.

"Of course not. But when you've invested a lot in your education, you expect certain outcomes."

"Which are...?"

*Oh, for heaven's sake.* The woman was like Saturday Night Live's David Spade. Would she trail off her every sentence into a lilting question? So you feel...? Because you are...? "My degree is in marketing, my job is marketing. Perfect fit."

"Well then, good." Dr. Adler smiled. "And Michael supports your professional goals?"

Libby would stick to the script Stephen outlined.

"Well, Michael and I come from different backgrounds. We bring certain expectations with us. It can get complicated. Misunderstandings... Our families clash terribly. It's a continual compromise. And...and Michael's very uncommunicative." My God, she should muzzle herself before she used up all their material.

"I understand." Another no brainer from the Ph.D. She then turned her attention to Michael and graced him with a beautiful smile. "Any thoughts on these problems, Michael?"

Libby stifled a laugh. There was no way her attempt at clever questioning would get anything out of him. Libby relaxed back, prepared to be entertained.

Michael hooked an ankle atop his knee, his expression thoughtful as he twirled the toothpick easily.

Then he slid it from his lips.

"I think our problems are mainly sexual."

"Ah..." The good doctor gave him a knowing smile.

# Chapter Four

Libby would simply kill him. That would give them plenty of material for this session.

"Are you upset by Michael's admission, Libby? Would you like to talk about it?"

"No."

Another knowing smile from the doctor as she steepled her fingers, looking at Michael over the tips of beautifully polished nails.

"Can you explain, Michael?"

"Well..." he said and then paused, drawing it out as though reflecting on his thoughts. "Libby's afraid to let herself go...and really respond to me."

The doctor nodded.

Libby resisted rolling her eyes as she watched his show of concern, his brow furrowed in bewilderment.

"She..." He pretended to struggle, rooting around for the right words. "She thinks too much, instead of just giving herself over to the moment."

"I see." Dr. Adler gave Michael a thoughtful frown and then rested her eyes on Libby. "Any response to that?"

Libby had to make some effort here. "Well, I suppose sex is more psychological with me." She snapped onto an idea. She would have Michael explain his scientific theory that he explained to her just this morning over breakfast — his theory of why he ended up on her side of the bed.

"Michael sees sex as more of a biological drive. Sweetheart, tell Dr. Adler about…how do you describe it? Your *'marking'* theory."

"Marking?" Dr. Adler's eyes lit up.

He leaned forward and propped his wrists on his knees. "It's the mating instinct where the male marks the female as his…at least physically. When he absorbs her scent and taste and responds favorably, he's then continually drawn to her heat, both consciously and unconsciously."

"I see," Dr. Adler said quietly.

His eyes grew intense, his voice low. "The male seeks to mate with her over and over until he has satisfied the drive. It's a stimulus/response reaction. The smell of her hair, the feel of her skin…he'll react." He shrugged. "Whether it's appropriate at the time or not."

"So you're saying, unlike Libby, the psychological factors don't have to be in place for you to respond to her sexually."

Libby was taken aback by the intimacy of the remark.

Michael shifted in his seat. "Yes," he said, his face growing dark. A muscle jumped in his jaw. It seemed the rough shadow of his beard was getting darker by the minute, as though the very nature of this talk brought out his maleness.

He continued. "The female responds, too. Once the male spills his seed and she absorbs it into her bloodstream she bonds with the scent of the male, she seeks him out too…to mate with, exclusively, until she's impregnated. In this way the male stakes his claim on her."

Michael's eyes were smoldering.

The doctor looked a little flustered. "Is...that an important part of this? Female impregnation?"

Michael's head snapped up. "What?"

The doctor folded her hands in her lap and smiled tentatively. "Have you discussed children?"

"Children?" Libby repeated weakly.

"Libby's wrapped up in her career," Michael snorted.

She took exception to his rash assumption and then almost laughed aloud at the absurdity. They were just playing a role. "I want children."

"Four?" Michael's eyes narrowed.

"Four?" Libby choked. "You can't be serious. Why...no woman can handle four children and a career."

"Like I said, she's tied to her career."

The doctor interrupted. "Well, I see we have some issues to cover next time—"

"Just because I don't want an entire preschool doesn't mean I'm tied—"

"Would you quit your job?"

Libby's mouth dropped. "I don't believe what I'm hearing. It's like a time warp."

The doctor leaned in. "It's best to refrain from judging—"

"Shut up," they said simultaneously.

"I'm not surprised." Michael jumped up. "I can just see it. My mother crying over another grandchild she doesn't get to see." He stormed out.

Libby watched, dazed, as the door slammed. She gave herself a moment to catch her breath. She didn't know what to make of his outburst. It seemed so real.

The doctor's soft voice penetrated her haze. "For a man who is uncommunicative, he did pretty well." She smiled sincerely.

Libby nodded and eased herself off the sofa.

"Your husband's a passionate man, Mrs. Meehan."

**\* \* \* \* \***

Terrell seemed restless as he sat with Libby for their little "getting to know you" exercise.

The pool was packed with couples stretched out along colorful chaise lounges that were set under large canvas umbrellas. The oppressive temperatures had abated and Libby was beginning to enjoy the dry heat and cloudless skies.

"Let's forget about this questionnaire, Terrell," Libby said to him. "How are you enjoying your fourth day at 'Camp Perfect?'"

"I'm not," came his quick reply. "I mean, if Belinda and I are supposed to be working on our marriage, why am I sitting here with you?"

Libby glanced at the dark skinned former wide receiver for the University of Chicago and then at herself. Something clicked, she just wasn't sure what.

"Terrell, how did you hear about this place?"

"We won this session through our gym at home. We're saving for a house and kids. We'd never spring for this on our own, plus..." He leaned forward. "We're not having any marriage problems other than the problem of this place keeping me busy with everyone but my own wife. Isn't Michael irritated?"

Libby glanced at Michael and Colleen sitting at their chaise lounges, side by side. He was stretched out flat, his mirrored glasses facing the sky while Colleen chatted with him, tipped on her side, questionnaire laid out on the edge as she bent forward to read it. Her ample breasts spilled over the delicately piped edge of her bikini and her lightly freckled face blushed with the pink rosy hue she'd gotten yesterday when their group golfed together.

Michael turned abruptly and flashed Colleen a bright smile. Then he actually laughed.

She wondered about his "male reactions" to her as she stretched out next to him. Was he marking her too?

"Time's up." The coordinator, a tall dark Latin looking man called out, coming up to their corner of the pool. "Let's gather around." He carried a clipboard and motioned for the waiter.

As their drinks were replenished and tiny sandwiches of shrimp salad and large wedges of fruit were served, Libby zeroed in on the other groups, searching for a pattern. The fact that she had no experience with marriage, other than watching her parents' dysfunctional arrangement, was a disadvantage. She'd have to circulate a little more. Tonight she would linger at the buffet stations and in the powder room.

\* \* \* \* \*

Large palm trees, weeping willows and poplars skirted the perimeter of the dome. As Libby and Michael strolled along, they stopped occasionally to attach miniature cameras and listening devices to the thick lower limbs of the trees.

"By the way," she commented. "Now that we're finally alone, I'd like to compliment you. That was quite an act in that therapy session."

His eyes narrowed and burned through her. The cords of his neck tightened.

She caught her breath. "You weren't acting?"

The hard line of his jaw grew rigid.

She tried to lighten the mood. "Well, good luck finding a woman who'll quit her—"

"I already have." His gaze impaled her. She glanced away, irritated that she'd mentioned it. She didn't want to get into a thing with him. Four kids, this whole marking theory, claiming his female and keeping her barefoot and pregnant. He *was* a Neanderthal.

Without warning he drew her swiftly to a thick poplar and caught her around the waist. Her pulse shot up and a light pounding started in her ears. He always moved in before she could protest, and now he attempted to press her against the trunk. But this time she was quick enough to thrust her hands between them and lay her palms flat against his chest to keep him at bay.

He dipped down to her ear.

"That's not necessary." She was quickly losing her patience. "Just place the damned bug." He felt like a rock wall under her palms and she had to fight the stimulating feel of him. While he reached above her head with one arm to snap the tiny instrument along the bark, he leaned in and slid his tongue around her earlobe, his hot breath warming her neck. She had judged him prematurely.

Neanderthal man was too sophisticated—he was more of a cave man.

His body heated against hers. Today he smelled of a light citrus cologne with a hint of sweetness. The rest of his scent was distinctly familiar to her, having slept beside him for three torturous nights—her lying beneath him was more accurate.

His scent. Humph. She was beginning to think like him, with this marking theory, and then for one appalling moment she found herself wondering about the gravitational thing he came up with today. He claimed they shared the same field and, like magnets, were continually drawn to each other, the gravitational pull of opposites attracting.

All she understood was that he grabbed her up at will and touched and stroked her all day under the guise of an attentive husband so that by the time she got into their pretend marital bed she was primed into a frenzy and strung tight.

She had to get him to stop this or she'd never make it the two weeks.

She pressed her knee between his legs and he groaned. She pressed harder and he stiffened.

"Done?"

"You bet."

* * * * *

Michael yanked on the antenna and dialed the lab as he paced their suite. Libby was doing her disappearing act into the bathroom for the fourth time now. He had come to expect her little routine. He liked that she was nervous around him no matter how cool she acted. He could feel it in the little pulse behind her ear and see it in the way her lips turned up at the corners in a forced show of relaxation while the set of her eyes betrayed her feelings.

She came out in a short one-piece number, the silky skirt full and flowing around her thighs. The halter-top shaped her breasts beautifully. No bra again. Damn, she was tempting.

"Michael?" The voice of the lab technician snapped him back.

"What's going on, Jack? Stephen tells me you guys haven't even run those prints yet. And what about the chips from the hard drive?"

"What chips?"

"Jesus. Are you guys all on vacation?"

"I thought there was no hurry. You two weren't supposed to break into rooms or anything. Just survey—"

"What the hell does that mean?"

"Libby knows."

He handed her the phone and dumped himself into the nearest chair. They shouldn't even risk this conservation over the airways, but he couldn't figure out the lab's delay.

Libby stood before him, turning slowly as she spoke. "Yes, but—"

He dipped his head and leaned closer, trying to see if she had stockings on and then saw the silky shimmer. He wanted to run his hand along her leg.

"I understand, but surely—"

When he stroked her knee she jumped and slapped at him. The silk swayed and he caught sight of lacy elastic at her thighs. Pure instinct had him lifting the hem of her dress for a better look.

"What in the world?" she snapped, flattening her hem and backing up. "What are you doing?"

Adrenaline shot through him at the glimpse of lace panties and matching thigh-high stockings. The urge to lay her on her stomach across the bed and cover her was powerful and immediate. This wasn't natural, this craving. He kept telling her he had no control over his responses to her. Trouble was, he was beginning to believe it.

She shot him a look of pure venom. "No, not you, Jack. This lunatic I've been partnered with."

Michael took a deep breath. Something had to give. If he could just fuck her once he was sure this lust would settle.

She scowled at him while she spoke into the receiver. "No, we're working out fine."

He studied her. She may be irritated with him but her nipples were erect. And the air-conditioner wasn't even on.

* * * * *

The dining room was a lively mix of races and ages. Not everyone was physically fit or attractive. And if jewelry and clothes were any indicators, a wide range of class was represented.

No pattern once again. Why then did Libby get the feeling the pattern was right in front of her, yet she couldn't see it? Like a camouflage.

The place must be run legit and used for money laundering. When the lab returned those codes from the hard drive Michael sent they would know more.

"Did you get any answer back on those prints?"

"Nope."

Libby frowned. "I haven't heard anything on the Doc's credentials, either. Maybe tonight."

Libby slipped off again like she had been doing all night, trying to dig up information while Michael covered for her.

Planting herself in the powder room got her more information than she needed but one thread kept popping out: the words "discount, free trial, coupon, trial offer" in addition to Terrell and Belinda's "winning session." She started counting; one in four ladies she spoke with had been "winners."

The other pattern was that they were all beautiful.

In following the conversation at their table that night she discovered that the doctor and his wife had been offered a complimentary stay in the hopes he'd refer patients to the facility, and Colleen and Sean were given a fabulous discount through their small business association.

The conversation at the buffet table revealed random discounts and offers and the only connection Libby could make was that all the "specials" were given to attractive couples versus the more plain.

But for what purpose?

* * * * *

"I'm just suggesting," Libby continued as she tugged at silken strands with her brush and then ran her slim fingers through the ends of her hair, "that you casually ask around. So far, on the face of it, I'd say about twenty-five percent of the couples are enjoying this free of charge — the exceptionally attractive ones, that is."

In that case, Michael thought as he gazed at her, they should be *paying you* to attend. He muted the TV. "I'll hang around the fruit bar outside the gym before everyone packs it in for the night." He eased himself off the thick comforter just as she disappeared into the bathroom.

She called after him. "Good."

As he grabbed the key off the night table he gave a final glance at the TV, finding it hard to drag his eyes away. Yankee's pitcher, Mussina, hit one down the pike. Maybe he'd just watch this inning. He heard the gentle pelt of water as Libby started the shower.

The first two batters struck out as Mussina continued to pitch flawlessly, as he had all night. Michael settled himself against the headboard and glanced at his watch. One more inning and he'd head out.

As much as he loved his job, he sometimes felt resentful about what he missed. He was supposed to be at this game with his brother and his son, Michael's only nephew. It hadn't been easy getting front row tickets behind the first base line. He would have liked to see ten-year-old Sean catch a foul ball first hand. And now it seemed, like Wells and Cone before him, that Mussina might pitch a perfect game.

Two outs, third batter up. Mussina threw a curve right over the plate. Nomar Garciaparra didn't even swing. Michael sat up straight and leaned forward.

Mussina fired another ball just as Michael's gaze riveted on Libby toweling her hair, head bent, as she walked slowly toward the dressing table. He hadn't heard the door open.

He swallowed hard. Nothing could have gotten him to turn back to the TV. Not even Mussina pitching against A-Rod.

Libby's naked form glowed in the lamplight, the gentle curves of her breasts and hips smooth and contrasting against the fine definition of muscle in her well-toned thighs and arms.

But what captured him was the sight of her large dark nipples, like peaked milk chocolate drops, on pale breasts that were small and delicately shaped, the contrast powerfully erotic. He thought of Hershey kisses, melting in his mouth.

His eyes dropped to the equally dark patch of softness glistening with moisture at the V of milk-white thighs. Lust shot through him with an urgency he couldn't ignore, his cock heavy and sliding down his pant leg.

He should say something but he couldn't respond in any way but the most elemental. She turned to the mirror, giving him a perfect view from the rear. Looking at the soft swell of her bottom drove him through the roof. He waited, hoping she'd bend over to pick up the brush and gave him a glimpse of her sweet pink pussy. He cursed himself for thinking it, but still didn't alert her to his ogling.

She dropped the small towel onto the chair and met his eyes in the mirror. What happened next could have lasted seconds or hours as time slowed while he savored every last glimpse of feminine softness and then sped up as she sought to deprive him by covering herself with the small rectangle of terry cloth. She pulled one edge over those delicious brown tips so he dropped his eyes to the soft tangle of curls. She tugged the bottom of the towel to the tops of her thighs.

They stared at each other, a Mexican standoff, her brown eyes wide and stunned, unblinking, while he blinked in astonishment, his mouth gaping.

"You..." she stammered. "You were supposed to be gone."

While she struggled for a scrap of dignity, he faced another dilemma. Should he tell her he was enjoying a gorgeous view of her squirming bottom, reflected in the mirror at her back?

He opened his mouth to speak, but before he could explain with an apology, she caught his rapid glances in the mirror and whirled around, realizing her mistake.

"Turn around," she screamed as she scurried to the closet, the towel too small to fully cover every tempting curve. She yanked a robe off the hook and in one swift motion turned away from him and threw it over her shoulders just before he caught the sight of her firm breasts swaying gently with the movement. She belted the robe and faced him abruptly.

If he had wanted to crack her glaze of self-composure, he had succeeded, but this was not the way he wanted it. She glowered at him, clutching her robe and shaking. He tried to think how to redeem himself. He had made no attempt to look away when she struggled to cover herself, and although there wasn't a red-blooded man in America who would question his behavior, he wasn't so dense that he didn't know she would see it differently.

"I hope you're pleased with yourself," she said coolly, striving for dignity despite the vulnerable position he had put her in. She walked quickly to the dressing table and yanked the brush through her tangled hair with a vengeance. "It certainly confirms my opinion of you as a

Neanderthal with no more manners than currently attributed to orangutans."

He'd recovered enough to slide off the bed but not enough that visions of her delicious body had receded. Like a camera's flash that explodes in the eyes, images of her clicked before him, the impression of silken thighs and dark ripe nipples indelibly etched in his brain.

"Libby." He walked up behind her. She stiffened, the brush stopping in mid-stroke before she resumed with greater intensity.

Her dark eyes seared into him from the mirror's reflection. "I'd appreciate you not broadcasting your find to your cronies in the Bureau," she snapped.

If he was insulted that she thought he'd engage in locker room talk like some horny teenager, it passed with the vulnerability he saw in the set of her mouth. Despite her haughty reprimand she was deeply shaken. He'd humiliated her, although he only half understood why. It was a mystery to him and most men, he was sure, why any woman would consider such blatant male admiration embarrassing. But of course, she would.

"Libby…" His voice sounded hoarse to his own ears. "I'm sorry, but listen, I'm the one who should be embarrassed."

She searched his expression.

"I guess I wasn't thinking too clearly…thinking at all, with all that blood deserting my brain for other places." His lips quirked.

She met his gaze, just a hint of softness reaching her eyes. She blinked once and then lowered her lashes. "At least you have enough sense to admit your juvenile behavior."

"There was nothing juvenile about it. It was an instinctive male response."

She snorted and then rose, heading for the door.

He frowned. "And if you remember, I predicted all this."

Her brow arched as she stood poised at the bathroom, a taunting gleam in her eyes. Apparently an awkward moment was not enough to break her stride.

"All this?" she questioned.

"Me and you," he drawled. "In this room, together, with fresh flowers and lace, sharing the same bed."

If he had expected some response to what he was intimating, he was wrong, and his hopes of seducing her faded further. Why didn't she understand this would be easier if they just allowed nature to take its course? He was a man, she was a woman. They could be here for weeks. At the rate the Bureau was following up on their leads, maybe months.

"We're attracted to each other. Why not give in to the impulse?" he asked, his voice low.

Not a flicker of tension revealed itself in those unfathomable eyes. With an indulgent smile, she shook her head and then disappeared once again through that damned bathroom door.

He vowed that before this was over, she would willingly give him the pleasure of undressing before him. And she would admit that she wanted him. In fact, he would prove it to her by morning.

# Chapter Five

Libby stirred in her sleep. Visions of purple buttercup-like wildflowers faded into a bed of springy green moss, sponge-soft and wet with dew. She groped for the scent of the morning foliage but it disappeared along with the flowers. Instead, she smelled the rich scent of soap and clean, male skin and then warmth traveled through her. In her mind she turned to the warmth and breathed deeply, imagining the rough male texture and how it would feel. But she couldn't see him, nor the meadow, or the flowers.

Her mind seized suddenly on the night before and in instant replay she saw herself completely naked before Mulcahy as his dilated pupils raked over her breasts and down her thighs. Her lids flew open and fixed upon his large masculine figure entwined with hers, his knee between her legs as she lay on her back and he on his side, his palm open and resting on her inner thigh while her legs sprawled out on the tangled sheets. His dark tousled head lay tucked under her chin and rested along her collarbone.

Her pulse picked up to a screaming pace as she tried not to breathe and awaken him. She had to get out of his embrace before he could gather her up the way he liked to in the morning, because after last night she wasn't sure she'd resist.

He was too disturbingly male and she was drowning in him, even beginning to believe in this magnetic field theory because his presence pulled at her continually.

His breathing was even and shallow, warm against her breast, his lips inches from the bit of lace covering her nipple. She tightened instantly, thankful he was sleeping soundly.

But then he stirred and burrowed further, his lips a breath away from the taut tip of her breast. Arousal stirred between her thighs and she groaned inwardly as his palm slipped farther up her leg, his fingertips resting on the lacy elastic of her panties. She throbbed in response, resisting the urge to squirm at the intimate ache growing quickly and snaking up her spine.

He moaned lightly, and then his breathing grew steady again.

She gazed at his sleeping head and at his lips, relaxed, and the strong set of his jaw, stubbled with growth. Involuntarily, she lifted her fingertips to trace the rough line of his jaw but hesitated, questioning the wisdom of it. She watched him awhile. He didn't stir. She loved the smell of him, clean and warm, a scent so distinctly different from hers. She would recognize it anywhere. With a soft groan, she chided herself for sounding like him with his marking theory. His scent stamped on her senses? Hardly.

Eventually she would wriggle from his grasp, but for now she studied the corded muscles of his shoulder and bicep and the bronze skin pulled tight over well-defined sinew. His hand felt large and warm against her thigh, causing nerves she scarcely knew she had to leap to the surface. She stirred instinctively and he responded by slipping his hand up over her panties to slide under her nightshirt and settle on the bare skin just below her navel. She held her breath, her heart pounding in her ears from the stimulation of his fingers sliding across her. What would it feel like to have his fingers slip beneath the lace?

She grew wet and full. This was madness.

With a gentle nudge she lifted his head with her shoulder and tried to slide him off. But like an infant disturbed from his nap, he rubbed his face and grimaced, his nose sliding along her nipple. The friction of the lace sent little jolts of sensation straight to her groin. She gasped aloud and panicked, the drowning feeling overtaking her. Never had she felt so out of control with a man. He simply consumed her bit by bit and she couldn't allow it. But he felt so good against her. His heavy frame was wrapped around her, his chest like a granite wall, indestructible, cradling her protectively. But it was an illusion. This man had the power to hurt her. He was only interested in one thing—her body, and she couldn't imagine why. She'd always considered herself too thin, small-breasted and pale. Surely he didn't lack female attention. Even she, for all her determination to steer clear of him, could hardly resist him.

"Michael?" She gave a harder nudge.

He groaned at being disturbed and rolled closer, drawing up his knee and pressing between her thighs. She arched to the sweet pressure that helped ease her ache. His hand stroked over her stomach and midriff idly, but his breathing told her he was in a deep sleep.

She wondered if he was dreaming about his Donna Reed clone who waited at home ready to quit her job to raise the kids. But before she pushed him off she'd allow herself this innocent indulgence of lying in his arms. As soon as he awoke she'd stop him.

She relaxed into the sensations and the feel of him. Of his lightly callused fingertips tracing along her hip bone, the friction alerting her every nerve as he traveled along the smooth swell of her belly and then up, stopping at the slope of her breasts.

She sighed in disappointment, her nipples aching for his light teasing touch.

He rubbed his face again in the lace of her bodice and then, as though he instinctively sensed there was more, he burrowed his nose in her cleavage and breathed in her scent. His lips followed and intuitively found the hardened nub of one nipple and brushed lightly. She sighed in contentment and then almost leaped off the bed as he attempted to draw it between his lips and suckle her. But he was still asleep; his eyes were closed and then his lips relaxed again. He nuzzled her sleepily and settled back into her breasts.

She stifled a sigh and drank in his smell, pondering her conflicting emotions. While she knew his dreams were not of her, she was sure his actions must be instinctive and that his body was unconsciously responding to hers.

As he continued to sleep, she waited patiently, her nerves lit and fiery. She prodded him.

He didn't move.

She moved her hips to slip his hand lower, wriggling a bit in an effort to stir him. If he woke up, she'd blame him.

He remained motionless.

She arched her hips to his knee and pressed, easing the ache but fueling the fire building within. Her restlessness increased but he was like a dead weight, his breathing regular while she was strung tight with sexual tension.

With a delicate aim, she jabbed her elbow lightly into his gut.

In response, he pressed the full length of his body along her side. Her tension went through the roof. His nocturnal erection was full and hard and pressing against her hip. She wanted to turn into him and wrap her leg around his waist, slip that hard strength into her, deep. The shock of her thoughts left her breathless.

No man had ever quite stirred her like this.

She was burning up and aching for his touch. She wanted to slip her hand between their bodies and stroke him. The thought brought a new rush of wetness between her legs.

She squirmed and turned onto her side, resisting the urge to touch him but no longer sane enough to practice restraint. His body moved with hers in a sensuous dance, easing up so she could slide her hips along his, the feel of his cock hard against the lace of her panties. It occurred to her that all that separated her from joining with him was a tug of elastic and the silk opening in his boxers. It was such a natural thought, a natural act, she didn't understand why she hadn't agreed with him before. Nothing mattered now but the heat of this primal rush.

She ran her hands down the hard planes of his chest, tangling her fingers in the curly mat of dark hair and then tracing over the ripple of muscle along his stomach.

She closed her eyes from the tent he made in his shorts and fought the urge to slip her hand under the waistband. She groaned audibly and wrapped her leg around his hip, pressing closer to him.

The feel of his fingers hooking around the lace edge of her bodice drew her attention sharply, and she gasped when he pinched her nipple between his thumb and forefinger.

His dexterity was not that of a slumbering man.

Her eyes flew to his face, but he ducked his head to her breasts and sucked hungrily. He had her stripped to the waist in an instant and flat on her back.

"Michael," she gasped.

He nipped gently at her nipples, first one and then the other, a breast cradled in each palm.

A long shuddering groan captured her, smothering the protest buried in her chest. And then the air left her lungs as she felt his fingers slip beneath the elastic leg of her panties. She moaned aloud as one long finger eased into her intimate depths. She was soaked.

"No," she blurted.

The gentle thrusting of his finger stopped and his lips stilled.

"Michael..." She drew her hips back, escaping his fingers, and then tugged at the thick tumble of hair at her breasts. He licked her nipple before she dug her fingers into his scalp and dragged his head up.

"Stop, Michael, please," she choked. This little game of hers had gone too far.

He propped himself on his elbow, his gaze beseeching. "Just let yourself go, Libby." A dark lock of hair fell over his forehead and a vision formed of him as a boy, his eyes pleading for another cookie.

She gave herself a mental shake. This was no boy, despite his baby blues. This was a man whose pupils dilated with passion and who was pressing her with the powerful evidence of his lust. She realized with a start that the smooth skin of his erection poked through his boxers and was stroking her thigh. He caught her hand and slid her fingers down his hot silky length.

In one panicked motion she leaped off the bed, dragging her bodice up around her and averting her eyes from his shorts. But despite her efforts, her gaze returned. He made no effort to cover himself.

He was magnificent.

"Come back to bed, Libby," he said, his voice low and vibrating with arousal.

It was now or never. If she hesitated to turn this bizarre incident around she'd be swept under by him, left with too much to regret.

She gazed into his eyes, dark with passion, the rigid set of his jaw tense and waiting. When he spoke, the deep timbre of his voice was like molten liquid dripping over her. "You know you want me."

"That's not entirely true," she clipped before she could think.

His brow arched. "You're hot and wet. Don't fight this, Libby." His voice was calm and low, almost reassuring.

Her eyes dropped to his shorts again. He was as large and thick as ever.

She tried to sound in control but her voice came out as a bare whisper. "Would you mind covering yourself?"

He grimaced. "Yes, but I guess I have to before you faint."

Why was that, Libby wondered, that he wanted her to look at him while she was mortified when he did the same?

As though answering her thoughts he said with a grunt. "Don't even try to figure it out." He had pulled the sheet to his waist but the hard ridges of his chest still taunted her. She had to get hold of herself and end this gripping paralysis. "Don't think of it as casual sex, Libby. Think of it as a natural attraction we can take pleasure in. This isn't your run-of-the-mill situation and the release of tension will keep us more alert and focused on our assignment." His eyes turned soft. "Come here."

"I'm not very good at it," she blurted.

He tipped his head, the blue of his eyes brilliant as the morning sun slanted through the blinds.

"At sex," she explained.

His lips barely parted.

She wanted to crawl into a hole for humiliating herself like this. What was she thinking to lay herself bare before him? Her problem was that she *wasn't* thinking.

"I see," he said. Then he eased himself off the bed and came to her.

She couldn't look at him and studied the carpet instead.

He cradled her chin in one hand and lifted her face to his. "Maybe you just haven't had enough practice."

If it weren't for the gentleness in his eyes, she'd think he was making fun of her. She felt an unreasonable urge to let him hold her.

But this was not a fantasy she could play out or a love story that promised a happy ending. This was Michael

Mulcahy, fellow agent, whose goals and values contrasted sharply with hers, who didn't even like her, and with a girlfriend at home. Or was she the one who said she didn't like him? Well, he hadn't denied it.

She stepped away carefully, not willing to take the risk, yet not ready to give it up. "I'll think about it," she replied.

His reaction was unexpected. He laughed, but not *at* her, because with a gentle touch he skimmed his fingers along her jaw. "Fair enough."

He grabbed his terry robe off the bedpost and called over his shoulder, "First dibs on the shower. I need a long cold one this morning."

\* \* \* \* \*

Michael studied the tall voluptuous brunette and her partner, who looked like an ad for Calvin Klein, as they waited outside Dr. Adler's office. He moved a miniature potted palm out of his way and picked up an issue of *Science and Technology.*

Libby elbowed him and motioned to the couple. "I'll bet they're here for free," she whispered.

He grunted. "You think he's good looking? He looks gay...too pretty." He ran his hand through his own scruffy hair in an involuntary gesture and frowned. It was getting too long; maybe he should get it styled. Then he shook his head at the thought.

"What about her?" she asked, looking up at him, her liquid brown eyes huge. "They must be double D's."

Michael shrugged and gave the woman a quick once over. "You couldn't even get close to her with those knockers, you'd be buried alive." His eyes dropped to the small claddagh necklace resting on Libby's cleavage, the one they pretended he gave her. He was imagining her delicately shaped breasts under the silky material. He didn't think she had any idea how beautiful she was.

She looked at him in surprise, and he noticed with astonishment the color that rose to her flawless skin. His Libby was losing her cool facade, chip by chip. His Libby? He shifted. "Ask them," he murmured.

In the space of a minute the couple was telling her their life story. They were enjoying a trial offer, compliments of their country club.

Dr. Adler floated in and handed the couple a packet. "You'll find the dome schedule in here. We look forward to working with you."

When they left she turned to Michael and Libby. "Ready?"

Michael groaned inwardly. He couldn't fall into the trap he got himself in last time. He didn't know why he reacted so personally when the doctor brought up children. Libby asked him tonight to steer away from introducing any talk of their sexual relationship. She had a theory that the doctor herself would guide them toward it. Connections between physical beauty, free admission and sex were cropping up and Libby believed Dr. Adler's therapy sessions played a part. The Bureau reported that her credentials came back as bogus. Today they'd get her prints. Even so, none of it added up to any connection with the drug cartel.

It wasn't long before the doctor got right to it. A few pleasantries aside, and she was pumping them for information on their sexual relationship.

Michael smiled easily. "Actually, Libby and I would like to talk about the children thing. Maybe her fear of getting pregnant is what's holding her back."

Libby nodded in agreement.

The doctor smiled back. "Normally I would agree to pick up there. But we have an unexpected opening in our special program and, since you mentioned past problems in your sexual relationship, I'd like to work you in right away."

Michael and Libby exchanged glances.

After a few weak protests, the doctor succeeded in sending them on their way, packet in hand, to the dome.

When they arrived at the odd-shaped building, they were surprised again that there were no windows in the dome. Because of this, the hidden cameras had picked up nothing but exceptionally attractive couples coming and going at all hours of the day and night. Now Libby and Michael were one of those couples.

An uneasiness settled over Michael. Before they entered, he turned Libby into his arms. Aware that there might be hidden mikes, he brushed his lips to hers and whispered, "Somehow I don't think any of this is connected with drug smuggling. I think we've stumbled onto an entirely different illegal operation. Since this isn't our assignment, we can drop this right now." The feel of her in his arms sent his blood pumping despite his sense of foreboding. He nuzzled her neck, a gesture that allowed her to whisper in his ear.

"Don't be silly. We can't be sure, and if something illegal is going on, we need to expose it."

He grew suddenly impatient and set her to face him. He spoke through his teeth. "I'm worried about the nature of this illegal activity. I'll understand if you won't do it."

"But you *will*, of course," she retorted.

He didn't understand her anger.

"It's part of the job," she continued, "and I'm up to it." She pinned him with a challenging glare.

"Fine. Anything for the job." He should have figured.

Upon entering the softly lit foyer, they were ushered into a plushly carpeted sitting room with a large stone fireplace.

As soon as they were introduced to their personal assistant, they were shown around the large facility that was filled with soft romantic music, wide-screen TVs and a variety of hot tubs. A masseuse was available upon request. They were encouraged to take a bath together before their therapy session, scheduled for the next hour. Before they could come up with a reasonable excuse, their attendant escorted them into a lovely room equipped with a king-sized bed, robes, towels and scented soaps and oils.

When their assistant closed the door and left them alone together, Michael let out a heavy sigh but didn't risk voicing his apprehensions aloud before he was sure the place was clean. If it was what he suspected, there would be cameras everywhere.

Libby had drawn aside the lace curtains of the sliding glass doors leading to the sunken hot tub. She had to be nervous, but he knew she'd put a stoic face on it. If she was anything, she was a professional. He had an idea how they could pull this off without blowing their cover.

He walked up behind her and, placing his hands on her shoulders, leaned into her hair. It smelled of lavender and soap and it felt like silk.

He pressed his lips against her hair. "I'll get in the tub first and wait for you. I'll pretend to doze until you're submerged. The scented bath crystals should bubble a bit and give you enough cover."

She turned to him and tilted her face to his. The relief in her eyes quickly turned pensive. "I can see a blinking red light in that painting facing the bed. I'm sure we'll spot cameras in the hot tub area, too."

He nodded and then looked at her, about to give her another chance to back out, but before he could, she strode casually to the bathroom. "I'll meet you in the hot tub, sweetheart," she called to him before disappearing through the door.

* * * * *

Safe in the bathroom, Libby stared at her reflection in the mirror. She hated this and began to shake with fury. If she were doing the job she wanted, she'd be interviewing a focus group on their opinions of the projected fall colors for women's jackets or recording male responses to perfume samples and then developing a marketing program. Instead she had to share a hot tub with a Cro-Magnon man who was devoid of any sexual inhibitions while surrounded by a roomful of cameras. It took all her will power to stay the tears gathering. She was so nervous she was shaking as she tried to summon the courage to join him. Although she appreciated the empathy she saw in his eyes, she had no idea what to do.

When she finally joined him, donned in her terry robe, he lay in a tub full of bubbles appearing relaxed and dozing just as he promised. She crouched down by the edge of the large tiled tub and dropped her robe before slipping under the water so quickly the cameras would have recorded only a bare glimpse.

He must have felt the subtle waves because minutes later he opened his eyes as she sat on the ledge across from him. His gaze was intense as he studied her, and although she knew he was only playing a part, her heart picked up a beat. He was so ruggedly handsome. While she buried herself in scented foam up to her neck, he was stretched out, arms relaxed along the tub's rim, exposed from the waist up. Of course, he was so tall and large, he'd have to sit on the tub's floor to submerge himself. She should be used to seeing him like this anyway—at the pool and then when he went to bed with just his shorts and nothing else. He was completely unselfconscious about his body. He had probably undressed in the room and walked naked to the tub. She glanced around. When she saw no robe, she concluded she was right.

Before she could wonder what was next, he lifted himself off the ledge and swam toward her, all glistening wet, muscled, 200 plus pounds of him. The thought that he was naked beneath the water sent her pulse racing. But she was being ridiculous. They wouldn't actually touch.

But he kept coming and then she watched in apprehension as he surrounded her. One large hand cupped her cheek and then he leaned in and kissed her in warm, teasing wet kisses that started a fire between her legs. His body so near sent her heart up into her throat.

He murmured against her lips, his fingers warm against her throat. "You're so delicious." He ran his tongue along her bottom lip, slowly, encouraging her to open her lips to him. But she didn't dare. What was he doing?

With the gentle tug of his thumb her mouth parted for him, allowing his tongue to slip in to caress hers in a mating dance that sent her nerves leaping to the surface. He was wet and rough and so male tasting. She pressed against his chest in an effort to push him away, but his heated flesh and the feel of his muscles, hard and unyielding under her palms, further fueled her tension. His skin felt taut beneath the muscle, both rough and smooth and so male, and covered with a light mat of hair. Before she could gather her sense he dragged his mouth from hers and began running his tongue along her throat. Didn't he remember the cameras? When he sucked on the throbbing vein at the base of her neck, she moaned with the tremors sweeping through her. His fingers gripped the tub's rim, effectively trapping her between his massive biceps.

"That's it, sweetheart, just give yourself over to me." She gasped when his wiry chest hairs brushed against her erect nipples. He gave a throaty groan.

Then he nudged her knees apart with his and leaned in between her legs. He was hard and pressed against her thigh. He murmured into her ear, "Yes, oh, God, you feel good."

Panic seized her. He was throbbing now, huge, and slipping up against the soft folds between her legs. Was he going to take her right here in the tub? Why didn't she do something? Before she descended into the dizzying sensual fog overtaking her, she gathered enough energy to stop him.

"Stop it," she said, pushing with what little she had. He backed up. "Don't touch me."

He straightened and stood. "Fine," he bit out. She stared at him, robbed of breath as he raged before her, fully aroused, every male muscle flexing with his agitation. His thighs were hard and beautifully sculpted muscle. But it was the power between them that she couldn't take her eyes off of. He was as beautiful as a Greek God, every pulsing inch of him. "Libby, look at me," he demanded.

She gulped. More like a Greek warrior.

"In my eyes."

Her gaze flew up to his, his eyes glinting with amusement. "This is exactly what I was trying to explain to Dr. Adler. No wonder she sent us here for therapy."

"What?" Dazed, Libby studied his face, trying not to let her eyes drop again. He must have seen her struggle because she caught his lips twitching.

Then he stormed out of the tub and the back view was almost as good as the front. With a backward glance before he disappeared through the double doors, he spoke to her, his erection like a flagpole jutting out from his stomach. "I'm sorry, Libby." His voice was soft and patient again. "I shouldn't have shouted at you. We'll discuss what happened in therapy."

Discuss it in therapy? Of course. Anyone viewing through the cameras the last few moments wouldn't doubt the authenticity of their actions. Hers certainly were real. She let out a mortified breath before he closed the door behind him.

\* \* \* \* \*

After a few days, Libby and Michael figured out the special sessions of the dome. At their first therapy session they were encouraged to try some sexual experimentation so that Libby could release some of her inhibitions. And while they were to practice these back at their suite, they were to discuss their progress in group session with other couples the next afternoon. They discovered that Terrell and Belinda had gotten roped into the sessions under the subtle pressure that they were to sample all the services as part of their "free" admission. Michael would bet that Sean and Colleen would be joining them soon.

This afternoon Michael noticed the obvious sexual titillation of the group as each couple's experimentations the night before were recounted. It had the quality of a sharing of sexual fantasies, and he was sure he knew where these were headed. He was also sure these unsuspecting couples had no knowledge of hidden cameras. Libby was an expert in detecting them and had counted five in this room alone: one in each corner and another overhead.

Poor Libby. While he found these sessions and their personal ones entertaining, she was always strung tight by the time they went to bed at night, no matter how many other activities they participated in during the rest of their day together.

And she seemed determined to try them all. She was a considerably good golfer and swimmer, and she enjoyed biking and the exercise gym just as he did.

Then there was always business to discuss each night. They debriefed each other on the findings from the hard drive Michael had sent to the lab. Accounts in the Cayman Islands and emails between the resort and two companies in Sweden led to connections between two underworld bosses. And fingerprints they'd lifted from glasses the staff had used traced back to criminal histories and numerous aliases. Libby's expert but discreet questioning of the guests pointed to the clientele as having been actively recruited rather than a random market of consumers.

The place was not what it appeared. The Bureau lab reports confirmed criminal records. The professionals on staff all had prior convictions. Yet, none were traced to the drug world. The common thread was their link to sexual vice: either prostitution or smuggling of censored material.

He glanced at Libby, sitting cross-legged on the lush carpet between two men. The group members were encouraged to mix—big surprise. The guy on her right resembled the Incredible Hulk; he was so muscle-bound Michael didn't know how he moved, and the other looked worse than a Calvin Klein ad; he was more like a Ralph Lauren model with his perfectly styled hair and coordinating designer clothes.

Libby looked...exquisite, and lately, so vulnerable. Probably because he reminded her every night by his actions if not with words how much he wanted her. And he continued to cradle her in his arms all night. He didn't know how he could keep resisting her. He wanted to snatch her from between those two guys ogling her. The Hulk even had the nerve to place his hand on her knee as they chatted before the session began. If Libby hadn't politely removed it, Michael would have dragged him off of her.

The voluptuous redhead next to Michael nudged him with her elbow. He peered down at the valley between her breasts. She was always paired with him and her tops were lower-cut each day. He was amused to discover she wore no bra and her neckline was loose enough for him to view the tips of her breasts from this angle—he was sure it was no accident. He suddenly realized that some of these "couples" had to be planted decoys. They must think he liked big-breasted women. Maybe if he wasn't so distracted by Libby this woman would interest him but right now he couldn't picture it.

"Your turn." The redhead smiled brightly.

They had gotten around to him. His mind scrambled to come up with some plausible thoughts on his and Libby's progress. He should have prepared something. Then he snapped onto a way to move these sessions along to their obvious goal.

"Well, Libby and I spent some time last night sharing our secret fantasies." He saw her arch a prim brow and he almost smiled, knowing she was bound to let him have it when they got back to their suite. But if he got the expected group reaction, he and Libby could expose more of these covert activities before the FBI stormed the premises. A fax came through last night that informed them the Bureau was getting ready to seize files and property. They were waiting on the search warrant. Since these operations weren't life threatening, getting the warrant had to wait until after the weekend. They had less than twenty-four hours now to uncover all they could.

"And?" One of the therapists, a tall slim blonde, encouraged him.

"Well…" His lips quirked. "I've always wanted to see Libby with three men."

A low murmur rose from the group and the men definitely looked pleased. Libby's gaze burned into him.

Michael chuckled. "What surprised me is how much she liked the idea." Before Libby could open her mouth he barreled ahead. "'Course, fair is fair, and she wanted me to do the same."

The therapist wasted no time in seizing on that idea and quickly surveyed the group. How did they feel about that? Did they find it stimulating? Most of the group was so inebriated it wasn't hard to get agreement. He began to wonder if more than alcohol was served. Since he and Libby were so "cooperative" no one noticed their lack of imbibing, but Michael made a mental note to remind Libby not to take a drop.

The group fell into an intimate discussion of their own sexual fantasies and more than one hand strayed as they lay sprawled along the rugs and couches before the dormant fireplace. The redhead had the nerve to run her hand up his thigh and cup his balls. He let her; what the hell? The Hulk's hand was back on Libby's knee and she was looking increasingly uncomfortable.

Shit. He'd look like an idiot if he objected now after he'd just told them how much they enjoyed the idea. The guy was stroking her knee and looking like he wanted to move up her thigh while she playfully tried to remove his hand. Then he dipped his head and nuzzled her ear.

Aw, hell. The session was almost over anyhow. Michael jumped up and scooped her easily into his arms, much to the Hulk's disappointment. Libby rewarded him with a grateful smile. As he swept out with her, he called teasingly to their little soiree, "See you tomorrow. Although I'm not much interested in talk."

# Chapter Six

Libby locked herself in their suite's bathroom, willing her nerves to steady as she pictured his large masculine frame sprawled along the soft lacy comforter waiting for her, although he would feign interest in his science journal. She needed to make a decision. In less than twenty-four hours their assignment would end, and she doubted she'd have another opportunity. Never had she been so drawn to a man.

She was not usually attracted to his kind of male arrogance, and she rebelled against the traditional attitudes he held. But she was drawn to him, nonetheless, and couldn't help fantasizing what it would be like to lay nestled within those strong arms, his weight pinning her to the bed, the feel of his raw strength filling her.

Then again, maybe she had convinced herself that the fantasy was better than the reality. That had certainly proven true in the past.

He was too large a man. She was overwhelmed by men in every area of her life. She didn't need to feel physically dominated, too. Yet his touch felt gentle in the way he'd skim his palm over her bare skin at every opportunity, which was frequent in this warm weather. She heated instantly with the contact, however casually executed, but if he noticed her response he gave no indication. He seemed to touch her unconsciously. His confidence was unsettling...everything about him was unsettling.

She knew she was skirting along a precarious edge with this man. There was every reason not to get involved with him, either physically or emotionally.

She wondered why he wasn't concerned about agency regulations that could get them dismissed from the Bureau if they indulged themselves. And she *wanted* to indulge herself in the most elemental way.

The thought erupted and excited her before she could censor it. She knew she could not get in that bed tonight and not touch him. And she feared when she awoke during the night, as she always did, that tonight she would not push him away. Why should she?

They were adults. They understood what they were doing. There was no reason to become emotionally tangled over a simple adult decision. She groaned at her cool logic. There was nothing dispassionate about her thoughts of him and no reasonable way to analyze it. He had set her on fire and she simply couldn't ignore her desire anymore. And she wasn't going to worry about next week or the woman he had at home. If he could keep this in healthy perspective, so could she.

Who had decided that women, unlike men, become emotionally attached once they had sex? A man no doubt.

When she came out of the bathroom in her satin slip of a nightgown, he was already in bed, wearing just boxers, his long bare legs on top of the sheets with the TV muted on some game and one of his science magazines propped open. It was uncanny how they had slipped into this nighttime ritual. She would slide in beside him each night, and he would subtly remind her that he wanted to make love to her, and then she would reach for her novel. Before they turned out the light, he would touch her "accidentally" several times, and her skin would burn in response.

When they finally retired, he'd wait until he thought she was asleep, and then he'd draw her up against him and hold her close. She loved the strong feel of him spooned behind her, skin to skin, his large hand cradling her waist. It always aroused him, but without a response from her, eventually she would feel him settle and hear his breathing slow. He had no idea how much she wanted him. He studied her without apology as she approached the bed. When she climbed in, she knelt before him and rested back on her heels instead of disappearing under the covers and waited for his subtle hint.

"Libby, if you're finished with your novel, I can suggest something better." He ran one finger through the side strands of her hair and studied her, the dark shadow of his beard a blatant reminder of his maleness.

She breathed in his scent, fueling her already restless desire. She drew a shaky breath. "Okay."

His mouth dropped.

"I warned you that I'm not very good at it."

He hesitated at first and then, without breaking eye contact, he dropped the magazine over the side of the bed, clicked off the TV and tossed the remote onto the nightstand. "All right..." He circled her waist and brushed his warm lips with hers, his eyes half-lidded and watching her.

She clutched his shoulders.

"Libby? Your nails are drawing blood." She was mortified when he gave her an amused frown and pried her fingers off him. He circled her wrists and pressed her palms against his chest. "Just relax."

Relax? Was he crazy? She concentrated instead on the muscled width of his chest, warm under her fingers, so wonderfully different. She couldn't stop herself from stroking along the hard ridges. He closed his eyes and smiled, so obviously enjoying the feel of her touching him. She thought of the way he never missed an opportunity to touch her, and how each time she had pushed him away. He was the most physical man she'd ever met. He wasn't the least concerned with the tent that had blatantly formed in his boxers.

He leaned back against the pillows, taking her with him. As though reading her thoughts, he clicked off the blaring intensity lamp. The soft glow coming from the exterior gas lanterns threw golden shadows over the sheets. His chest gleamed bronze under her palms, the wiry mat of hair like a dark shadow covering all those chords of muscle. Even his flat nipples looked tempting. Why didn't she just reach down and lick them?

He tipped her chin up. "You look like I did before I took my graduate exam for Johns Hopkins."

She startled at the comparison. "The graduate school exams were easy compared to this." She clenched her hands and sat rigid.

He let out a bark of laughter and bounded off the bed. She wondered for a startled minute if he had decided to forget it. Then she watched him lift two wine glasses from the cabinet.

"Libby..." His voice gentled as he tilted the wine carafe. "I don't know what kind of men you've been with, but I can guarantee you won't be *working* at sex tonight."

She diverted her gaze from his erection, but it was hard, knowing now exactly how he looked. In fact she remembered everything about him, the thick angry-looking veins that ran the powerful length and the dark dusky thickness. As he sank down beside her and handed her the stemmed crystal she worried suddenly that he'd be too big for her. Her fingers shook as she clutched the fluted glass and drank with an unsteady sip. It had been so long and she'd had so little experience. She probably drank too fast but she was anxious under his probing eyes.

He gave her a considering look. Stretched out lazily, he leaned against the headboard, drinking his own glass and watching her over its rim. When she was nearly finished, he placed his glass on the nightstand and ran his palm along her thigh, the tips of his fingers nudging playfully under the hem of her nightgown.

The contact was electric. She could see that he felt it too. The wine had gone straight to her head, making her want to spread her legs for him so he could reach where she was heating up so quickly that it took her breath away. She swallowed. And couldn't get her herself to do it. When she didn't open for him he trailed his fingers over the silk and up her belly and then cupped one breast through the slippery cloth. "A perfect fit." He smiled.

And then he sat up, took her glass from her, and stripped her to the waist in a move so smooth it hardly registered until his lips were on her. He groaned as he sucked one nipple between his lips.

"Like sweet chocolate drops," he moaned. She gasped with the responding pull between her thighs and suddenly grew restless for his touch. As though he sensed it, he slipped his hand under her nightgown and tangled his fingers in the soft curls between her legs, inviting her to open for him. On a soft sigh of surrender, she did. It was heaven. The blunt tip of his fingers circled her tiny bud and squeezed gently. She thought she would jump off the bed with the contact.

"You've been hiding from me, Libby," he growled, slipping his fingers all over her wet lips. He slid one long finger into her dripping pussy and she shuddered. "You're soaked and throbbing. I don't think you're going to last long, darlin'."

He pulled on her nipple and sucked hard. Just when she thought she couldn't take it anymore, he turned her around, settling her between his legs, her back pressed to his chest. His wiry hairs brushed along her skin. He breathed into her hair. "God, you smell delicious. Let's just relax and enjoy this."

But she couldn't relax, she was strung so tight she thought she'd go crazy. She wanted him inside her. Her heart picked up to an alarming pace. He caressed her breasts, cradling her and wetting her nipples with her own juices. His low masculine groan vibrated in her ear. "I think we should approach this scientifically," he said.

*What?* She was going to kill him. "Michael—"

"Shh..." he murmured into her ear. "I want to watch you come." He leaned her back against him and spread her legs wide in a gesture so lewd and unladylike that she thought she would die. But she didn't. She became incredibly aroused instead at the way he looked over her shoulder and watched himself play with her sex. She watched him, too, and grew fascinated. Her lips were so red and swelled. He separated her gently and smoothed her wetness everywhere in a touch too gentle to ease the ache but enough to torture her mercilessly.

She wanted him. Inside her, everywhere. The thought overtook her. She arched into his hand. "Please, Michael."

"Please, what?" he breathed, his hot breath fanning her throat. "Tell me what you want." He left her burning center and played with both her nipples.

She couldn't. She had no words to describe the desperation she felt. Why was he doing this to her? He tugged on her nipple, teasing the tingling bud with the rough pad of his thumb. She cried out in small sobs that broke from her lips.

"Michael," she choked, grabbing his wrist.

"Do you want me to fuck you?"

She turned crimson and nodded.

"Say it," he breathed.

She couldn't, wouldn't. She wanted to beat him for torturing her this way. When his hands slipped down between her legs, she sighed with relief. He petted her until she thought she would die.

"You've never been naughty, have you, Ms. Vandermark?"

He slipped a wet finger down between her buttocks. She gasped with the shock of him resting his finger at the tiny entrance to her bottom.

"Stop that, Michael."

"I will if you tell me what you want."

Her words of protest drowned in her throat when he gently squeezed her clitoris and then stroked. He spread her wider. Her little bud was starkly visible and throbbing, begging for release. He nipped her earlobe and probed her bottom. Panic and arousal seized her. She didn't recognize the primal moan that came from her own throat.

He smiled against her cheek. "Yes, we'll just let nature take over." He plunged his finger into her bottom. *Oh my*

*God.* The burning shock turned to pure pleasure as he stroked inside her. Then he slipped another finger into her sex and rubbed his thumb over her clit. She was lost. Strung too tight from days of his teasing and touching her and now she was responding with alarming swiftness. She rocked against his hand shamelessly, hoping she would finally discover what it was like to lose control.

"Shall I stop?"

"No!" she screamed. Pleasure rolled through her and gathered. His thumb circled her tight clit and pressed.

"Michael, I..." Her words drowned on a strangled cry.

"It's okay, Libby," he coaxed her. "God, you're beautiful. Just let yourself come. We've got all night."

"You don't understand—" She moaned, deep in her throat, gripping his forearms, her nails digging into his skin as she reached higher, until she exploded. Heat coursed through her body with a swiftness that shook her to her core, the fierce trembling frightening and wonderful. It was like nothing she'd ever experienced. Now she understood what other women knew. The pleasure that swept through her body and filled her with heart-pounding bliss was exquisite, enough to bring her to tears. She came completely apart, dissolving into a boneless liquid fire that melted every muscle. She collapsed on one long shuddering groan that left her limp and helpless against his chest.

"Well, I'll be damned," he muttered and then murmured endearments that she couldn't understand. "You've never had an orgasm before, have you?"

She shook her head, no. How could he have known? Was she so blatantly inept?

He pressed his lips against her forehead and smoothed the hair off her damp skin.

Before she realized what he was doing, he had laid her on the sheets and was dragging her nightgown down over her hips. He tossed the ivory satin over the side of the bed and then knelt between her legs. He rocked onto his heels and just looked at her.

"You don't know how many times I've pictured you like this." He ran his hands down her length, from her shoulders to her breasts, skimming over her hips and down her thighs.

In an impatient rush, he shoved his silk shorts over his hips and yanked them off. She slowly registered his size, thick and full, and standing now at rigid attention as he ripped a foil packet and then smoothed the condom down his length.

His gaze slid along her body, one hand settling between her legs. He nudged her thigh. "Open for me, Libby," he said, urging her to spread her legs, his voice rough with need. All sense of modesty had long fled and she felt she'd do anything he asked now.

But she was not prepared for what he did next.

She watched in tantalizing shock as he settled his face between her legs and with infinite gentleness separated her with the tips of his fingers. And then he tasted her, savoring her with slow sweeps of his tongue and stroking her with his fingertips as he did.

Never had she felt so vulnerable and womanly than she did watching him worshipping her sex. She felt a new urgency, more powerful than she had just experienced. When she writhed restlessly, he only increased the pressure. But she didn't want to climax without him. She wanted to feel him filling her and feel *his* pleasure.

"Michael, please. I want you." Her words sounded like a sob, and she worried that he'd think her melodramatic. This act that he considered simple biology was taking on more significance than she should allow.

He ran his lips up her body, stopping at her nipples and swirling his hot tongue over the hardened tips. "You're delicious," he murmured, sucking her gently and then burying his lips at her throat. When he settled himself between her legs, he was trembling with need.

"Please, Michael." She urged him with her hips, spreading herself and clawing to get him closer.

He reared up on his elbows and looked at her, his expression not what she expected. Mixed with his lust was an anxiety she couldn't identify. He shuddered when the tip of his erection nestled between her swollen lips and her folds gently separated and opened for him. The worry across his brow increased. She felt herself falling into the unfathomable depths of his troubled gaze.

When she smoothed her palm over the rough edge of his cheek, he turned his lips into her hand.

"What's wrong, Michael?"

"Draw your knees up." His voice shook with arousal.

When she opened herself to him, he slid in, hard and full and deep. She cried out when he rested against her womb and then reached instinctively to draw him closer, but he reared back and looked at where they joined, hip to hip, buried deep within her.

His brows drew together. "God," he breathed. He arched his neck, closing his eyes with a look on his face that resembled pure pain. His biceps quivered with tension. Then he eased up farther, hitching his knees under her thighs and wrapping one arm under her hips and lifting her. "I can't get deep enough," he groaned more to himself than to her.

She worried that he was too big and then wondered if that was even possible. He looked deep into her eyes and withdrew fully. He kissed her chastely on the lips and then thrust hard, once and then again, burying himself to the hilt and twisting himself inside her at the end of each powerful thrust, and then repeating it with an urgency that drove her to pleasure that was so sweet and all-consuming, she wanted to cry. She clutched at him, his body now slick with sweat and shaking, as he took her over and over again. She screamed with the explosion that reverberated through her.

With one last deep thrust he growled to himself, "I'll never get deep enough," and released all his need and tension into her in one long shattering groan.

Then all movement stopped. The only sounds were the beating of their hearts.

They were fused. As though they had melted into each other with no barriers between them. He breathed heavily. She ran her fingers through his thick hair and down along his sweat-skimmed torso, breathing in the rich male scent that she'd come to love.

"That took the bite off, but it's not going to be enough," he murmured hoarsely. He groaned and muttered what sounded like a curse and then withdrew from her, ripping off the condom and then tossing it on the floor.

Then to her amazement, he grew larger and harder again. He knelt up, looking angry with himself and so vulnerable. He was stiff again. He ripped open another condom.

"Turn over, Libby," he said, his voice a rasp. He ran his hands down his face.

The image of herself lying on her stomach stirred her own desire and then she groaned at the feel of him palming her bottom. He drew her up on her knees and took her from behind with an insistence that belied his explosive orgasm of just minutes before. And she responded in kind, shocked that he could incite her once again to the point of begging for him.

Still it wasn't enough.

After a brief half-sleep, he sat her on his lap facing him but he didn't move. He stimulated her nipples until she shattered around him. Then he took her as though they had never joined, so desperate seemed his need to bury himself inside her softness and take her over and over again.

Some time in the early morning hours they collapsed into each other's arms and slept.

# Chapter Seven

Libby shifted against the cool sheets, feeling the heavy warmth behind her. Michael's large hands encircled her and began their relentless stroking of her heated skin. His lightly calloused fingertips aroused every one of her nerves from their sleepy slumber. In perfect synchronization with the early morning hours there was a gentleness about him this time, a contentment.

She burrowed against him, loving the feel of him growing hard and sliding along her bottom. She knew he was half asleep while he slid his hands over her breasts and cradled her tenderly, but his body was awakening. When she lifted her leg, draping his hip, she felt his hardness pressing, instinctively seeking entrance. She whimpered restlessly.

He groaned and eased into her. And then he took her slow and easy, dropping soft kisses along the nape of her neck, teasing and torturing her with slow deep strokes in a comforting rhythm that held her protectively. They climaxed together, and the slow build-up was oddly reassuring, as though they had all the time in the world, forever. It was her last thought as she turned into his arms and laid her head against his chest. She drifted off to sleep with the feel of him threading his fingers through her hair.

\* \* \* \* \*

Libby felt his absence before she saw his silhouette profiled against the dawn light, his arm bent and leaning across the top of the window frame, peering out over the grounds. The glow from the lamppost streaked across his furrowed brow indicating that it was not yet five o'clock. He was smoking a cigarette, his concentration fierce. In the six months since she had transferred to his department, she had never seen him smoke, and she was sure he never had.

He cut a powerful figure as he stood, semi-nude, his hard-muscled chest and biceps flexing with the movement of fingers to lips as he drew deep on the tobacco.

Thoughts of the night flooded her as she watched the tensing of his granite jaw, remembering his tension during the night and then his total loss of control in her arms. How he clung to her and held her, only to start all over again. A warmth, so deep it melted her bones, traveled through her.

"Michael?"

His head snapped her way as she struggled to a sitting position against the pillow. Hoping he would come back to bed, she gazed at him in invitation.

His eyes dropped to her breasts. But then he ran an impatient hand through his hair. "This was a mistake." He tamped out his cigarette in the potted cactus and continued to look out over the landscape.

She instinctually clutched at the sheet and covered herself, desperately hoping he meant this assignment but fearing the worst. "You mean our insinuating ourselves in the group?"

"I mean you and me." He pinned her with a hard look, his expression implacable.

For one naive moment she thought he was testing her, awaiting her denial and then her reassurance about last night. But this was not a man who needed reassurance about his sexual prowess, or about anything.

She knew her voice would betray none of the emotion she felt even before she spoke. And she suddenly hated that part of herself: the unruffled coed turned slick FBI agent that served her so well, yet denied who she was. She wanted the Libby of last night, the one who burned in his arms, all poise melted under the heat of their passion and in the way she gave herself to him with total abandon, open and trusting, her soul bared.

She stifled a cynical laugh.

Now he didn't want her. But the irony did nothing to deaden the anguish gripping her insides and the pain that seared straight to her heart.

Nevertheless, she responded with the cool detachment she had perfected. "What is it? You still blame me for your partner's transfer?"

He looked at her in surprise and shook his head. "No. I found out about the gambling when you did. You were right to tell Clark before he got himself and the department in real trouble. He's working things out now."

"Then why did you tell Clark that you wouldn't work with me? Did you think I was incompetent?"

He scowled at her. "Incompetent? You're one of the best agents I've worked with. Why would anyone think you're incompetent?"

"Then why?"

He sighed. "It doesn't matter anymore."

She should have screamed at him, told him that he had no right to make love to her with such passion and then dismiss her so callously, but when she looked at him with his thick dark hair falling over his forehead and at the rough stubble of his beard all she could think was that she wanted to dissolve into his arms and beg him to say that he hadn't meant it.

But she did none of that. Instead she swung her legs over the side of the bed, taking the sheet with her. "There *is* no you and me, Michael."

He loomed up swiftly and grabbed her shoulders. "What was last night?" His eyes flamed, challenging her to react.

How dare he do this? Toss her aside and then expect her to — what? Congratulate him on his expertise?

She remained unperturbed and simply lifted a brow. "Biology. Nothing to concern yourself over."

She tried to move but he held her in a death grip, his eyes darkening with fury. "That's not what I saw last night when you screamed, begging me."

She jerked in his arms and he released her just in time for her to slap him, hard, across the steel set of his jaw. She returned her own furious glare, her words biting. "As you said, that was a mistake."

He stood rooted to the floor. A muscled jumped in his jaw. "You're lying." His words were barely a whisper.

Why was he doing this? Hurting her beyond what she thought possible? But she would not cry. She would not fall apart and confirm to him that she was, after all, just a woman, prone to irrational outbursts and emotional instability. Hardly someone who could be counted on to remain cool under pressure.

She struggled out of his grip and then turned on her heels and swept toward the bathroom door. Her only show of emotion was that of her closing the door a little harder than necessary.

It was only when she knew she was safely inside that she allowed her tears to flow and to feel the pain bottled so tight. She slid to the floor with her back to the bathroom door and held herself protectively, furious with herself at the same time for being so stupid. And then she felt the warm sticky moisture seep down her thigh.

For several frightened moments she tried to make sense of it. Her mind whirled to the last time he had made love to her...had sex with her...and then calculated the days since her last period. She tightened with panic. Just when she thought things couldn't get any worse, they did.

\* \* \* \* \*

Michael glanced up again at the clock on the wall above the group facilitator's head. He was sick of this suffocating togetherness and this whole assignment. And although he knew the Bureau would contact him if any home emergencies came up, he always hated the long periods away from his family. While his three younger brothers lived in New York and tried to look after their mother, they were still caught up in trouble left over from their divorces, and their struggles to see their own kids were endless. His widowed mother depended mostly on him. He wondered in irritation where the team was.

Just this morning, the Bureau had confirmed that the evidence that Michael and Libby had collected—the bogus credentials and fingerprints that proved the professionals had criminal records—was enough with which to go to the Grand Jury. The agency was ready to make arrests and seize records. Michael suggested they hit the dome first. He shifted with impatience when the clock struck three.

He had hoped it would be today, because there was no telling what was planned for their little group, and he was already fuming as he watched the Ralph Lauren gay guy fawn over Libby, although, apparently, he wasn't gay.

"Terrell and Belinda," the group leader purred. "You haven't shared yet."

Michael could see the tension in Terrell's neck. It was the tension a quarterback would easily recognize in his wide receiver. Either the liquor the group leader had been plying them with had yet to affect him or he was purposely monitoring his consumption, as were he and Libby. But aside from them and Terrell's wife, Belinda, everyone else looked shot.

Michael didn't know how long Terrell would last before he blew, but he hoped he could maintain just a little longer. Enough to get some solid evidence as to what the real purpose of this little retreat was. The Bureau could probably count on Terrell and Belinda testifying when the time came.

"We're going to try something new," the facilitator chirped on. "A team building activity involving trust." She quickly paired off the group into couples. He wasn't surprised when he was put with the redhead and Libby with "Ralph."

Ralph was so looped that Libby was successful so far in keeping his hands off her and while the redhead beside him pawed him continually, she'd need his cooperation to get anything going and that was *not* about to happen.

The leader was looking at Michael with suspicion. Libby and Michael didn't need to tip him off to something amiss this close to wrapping up the case. So, they had better get with the program.

He gave Libby a silent message, cutting a quick glance to the group leader at the same time he turned to the redhead and laid his palm on her thigh. Out the corner of his eye he could see that Libby immediately understood. Still, it irritated him when she touched her long, tapered fingers to Ralph's chest and smiled up at him.

The group leader's attention was diverted to the youngest couple paired up in the group. And suddenly the lights went dim and soft music filled the air.

"It's ow…kay, honey," the man on the redhead's other side called to his wife, his words slurred and confused. Michael began to suspect that something had been added to the liquor. "I want to see you get durned on by nother man."

Apparently, it was all the encouragement the young man needed. When the kid slipped his hand under the girl's short flared skirt, his own wife, who watched on, gasped from the sidelines. But other than whispering his name, she did nothing to stop what was about to happen.

Michael looked on in fascination. The girl was full-figured, with a low-cut Lycra top that showcased her cleavage. The kid tossed up the girl's skirt. "Let's *see* if you're turned on," he said, slipping his hand into lacey panties. When his fingers found home and thrust, she gasped. He pulled out, her juices all over his fingers, and licked them. "Oh, yeah," he groaned.

In one quick movement, he slipped her panties down to her ankles, causing the roomful of men to groan audibly at the glimpse of glistening pink pussy. Despite the fact that Michael knew the couple would probably be mortified when they sobered up and saw the tape, he felt his cock rise. Besides, he rationalized, they needed this kind of evidence. Michael was not about to stop the show.

He knew Libby felt the same way. The delicate vein along her throat was jumping, and he bet her pussy was getting good and wet. She *was* aroused. He could see it in her nipples, pulled up taut against the thin fabric of her dress.

Even in her unease, Libby was beautiful. Her eyes widened as she stared at the sight before her, seemingly unable to take her eyes off the writhing couple. The girl was unsuccessfully trying to pull her skirt over her pussy, but now that she was naked beneath, the kid was not about to let her. While he stroked up her thigh, flirting with the hem, the girl was turning crimson. Then the kid slid her down gently to recline on the carpet and knelt between her legs. He spread her thighs wide.

Libby turned as crimson as the girl, and the memory of how Libby looked when *she* was naked and aroused rose up to torture Michael. He didn't know what aroused him more, the memory of how sweet her pussy tasted or the look on her face when he licked her.

He smiled to himself. She really needed to indulge more. But then he frowned, since she wouldn't be indulging with him and he didn't like the idea of her indulging with anyone else, either.

The leader was droning on about the importance of satisfying our spontaneous passions or some bullshit to which no one listened, their attention instead claimed by Ken and Barbie as they lay spread out along the carpet. Ken had completely stripped Barbie now and was pulling one nipple and then the other between his lips. She was moaning and grabbing for his zipper like she couldn't get his clothes off fast enough.

He did it for her, standing up and stripping fast. It was the women's turn to gasp. His dick was so erect, it flattened against his stomach. Michael wondered how long the kid would last.

When he dropped down beside his partner again, he didn't waste any time getting her onto his lap. He plucked at her nipples with his teeth. Michael had to admit that they were fitting specimens for this little sex show. She was plenty curvy and her nipples were deep red and ripe-looking. As she smoothed her palms over Ken's bare chest she ground against his lap, her breasts bouncing with the movement, and then reached down to run her hands all over his cock. Michael could see the kid fighting for control. The veins on his neck bulged.

The girl cried out at as he continued to bite her nipples, but when she rose up and positioned herself over his cock, the kid stopped abruptly and lifted her off his lap. He turned her to kneel on all fours. Michael sat up straight, riveted. Other than the music the room went absolutely still, as though everyone was holding their breath.

Why not? Michael wanted to see the kid's cock sink into that soft, wet, waiting pussy just as much as everyone else.

She wriggled her bottom at him and cried out her impatience but for some reason Michael couldn't fathom, the kid hesitated. He reached below and coated his fingers with her and then slid one long finger up between her bottom cheeks.

Michael smiled to himself when he realized what the kid was up to. Probably more than he was ever allowed to be up to with his own wife. Michael couldn't blame him. Why waste an opportunity? The kid probed her bottom with his wet finger.

She rebelled and pulled away from him but he locked his hands onto her hips and pulled her back against his cock. She moaned when he slid his fingers down to pet her sex and then returned again to probe her bottom hole. Before long he had her moaning and crying in his arms and begging him to fuck her. Michael could only wonder what the poor girl was going to do when the dust settled tomorrow. But for now he just settled back and enjoyed it.

When he glanced over at Libby, she was as riveted as he.

The kid slid his cock into the girl's welcoming pussy and then plunged his thumb into her bottom hole and wriggled it. Within moments the girl was shuddering in his arms in an explosive climax. Then he pulled out suddenly, positioned himself at her bottom, and applied pressure. Before she knew what was happening, he was buried an inch. She turned and made a small protest over her shoulder, but the rest of his dick sunk easily. When he was in her bottom completely, Michael couldn't stifle the groan that rose from his own throat. His cock was bursting, but nothing could get him to look away from the rhythmic thrusts with which the kid rendered the girl's bottom. He looked like he was being tortured. In seconds the kid pulled out and then exploded in a powerful climax of his own, spurting his come along her bottom cheeks.

Michael could feel Libby looking his way. When he met her gaze, she swallowed convulsively and turned away, but for Michael there was no mistaking the fevered pitch in her eyes. If the agency didn't come soon, Michael was going to spontaneously combust.

When he glanced around, he was sure he would. The scene and the liquor and possible drugs had reduced everyone but he, Libby, Terrell, and Belinda to sex-crazed addicts. Each person was peeling their clothes off faster than the other and groping for any T & A that presented itself. It was getting out of hand.

Then Libby's partner made the irreversible mistake of sliding his hand well up under her skirt. All rational thought fled as Michael watched the guy slide his hand under her panties to stroke her backside. He ate up the distance between them in two long strides and yanked the guy up by his collar. "Leave your hands off my wife," he gritted through his teeth just as doors burst open and agents flashed badges and surrounded them.

Within minutes, the group leader and her assistant were cuffed, leaving the rest of the group to look on in stunned silence. It was a chore for the agents to get the inebriated group to understand that they were to put their clothes back on. Too many simply collapsed onto the carpet, now obviously doped up. They called for medical back up.

Once medics arrived, Belinda was the first to bombard whoever would listen with questions as the resort staff was led away. Libby quickly identified herself and Michael as agents. She told everyone who was conscious that they would be required to stay within the compound for questioning, but from here on their schedules were their own. After several moments of bewildered silence and more questions, there followed a low murmur of approval and they filed out. The rest were carried out on stretchers.

When Michael and Libby were finally alone, he stepped up and turned her to him before she could leave.

She drew back but gave him her attention.

"We have to talk," he said, gazing down into those liquid brown eyes that masked all emotion.

"About what?"

"Last night," he answered, not knowing where to begin. His mind had been reeling since he mentally matched the number of condoms littering the floor with the number of times he had made lo—had sex with her.

"There is nothing to talk about," she said stiffly, gesturing to move, but he caught her wrist. She grabbed at his hand to pry him off, but he wasn't budging. He had to know, even if it confirmed the worst. He didn't think a woman who was so sexually inexperienced was using any birth control regularly.

"Last night we had unprotected sex one time." He hated the clinical way he described an act that had taken on enough significance that it had been his undoing. He couldn't turn the clock back but he couldn't touch her anymore, either.

Her shoulders slumped, her cool facade slipping. She nodded.

"Do you use anything?"

She looked at him from down the slim bridge of her nose, her composure back. "No."

"Oh. Well, then we might be in trouble." He gazed upon her delicate features that for just a moment revealed the turmoil she felt. Remembering her warmth with him last night, he suddenly realized just how much it cost her to maintain her cool air of professionalism.

As the thought settled, he noticed her expression change as though she was on the edge of saying something. But then she glanced away and her mask was back. "I'll keep you apprised if anything turns up?"

"If anything turns—" He gave a snort.

She turned on her heels and headed quickly for the door.

# Chapter Eight

Libby hesitated before exiting the cab that had stopped before her parents' penthouse on East 74th and Lexington in Manhattan. The train to New York had given her too much time to think about her potential dilemma, and she thought now of her parents and their long held desire for a grandchild. Even with her three brothers in their late thirties, they still waited. She felt guilty for her thoughts over the last few days. She had more than ample financial resources, parents who, after the initial shock, would welcome a baby with open arms and, no doubt, three brothers who would relish their roles as uncles.

After the intense eleven-day assignment, followed by a quick debriefing, she and Mulcahy were both given a few days off to regroup. Just eleven days with him and one night of lovemaking, and he was indelibly stamped on her heart—her brain—and now might be intertwined with her life forever.

She couldn't seem to think of her potential pregnancy in purely clinical terms. What kept surfacing instead was the thought of a daughter, striving for the stars and looking to her mother for encouragement. Reluctantly, Libby admitted that she wanted to be that mother and give this child a chance. She gave herself a mental shake. Her agonizing might be over nothing.

The moist heavy air clogged her lungs for just a moment before Carlos greeted her warmly and ushered her through the thick glass and brass double doors. As the elevator slid up sixteen floors, she told herself to put out all thoughts of "what ifs" and try to enjoy the evening. Her father had some news he wanted to share with the family so all her brothers would be at dinner.

She fit her key into the thick mahogany door and braced herself for the onslaught of testosterone. She really didn't know how she and mother had survived. Years ago she had decided to abandon her mother's acquiescence and accommodation for a bolder strategy, but recently she had become exhausted with the struggle. All it had gotten her was a job that she really didn't want.

Before she could swing the door closed, her mother rushed to her side, calling for their butler. "Put that bag down, dear, and let Rahoul take it. You must be exhausted from your trip and this heat. Come, I'll get you some chilled white wine."

Libby found herself in her mother's warm protective embrace, enjoying the feel of her slim bejeweled fingers lovingly brushing the hair back from her crown, and for one horrified moment Libby thought she would cry. How incongruous that would be for Libby and how wonderful for her nurturing mother to give comfort to the daughter who never seemed to need it...or didn't until now.

Libby reluctantly allowed her mother to usher her into the "pit," the sunken living room where the males were hovered around the wide screen TV watching yet another endless game. How many years had she hid the remote or stubbornly stood in front of the screen annoying them?

So intent were all four men as they stared at the TV, murmuring instructions, that they didn't notice her enter. At the sound of a crack, her attention was drawn to the screen while the men let out a cheer and leaned forward, their concentration further heightened, if that were possible. A player in a white and red baseball uniform was running, his fitted pants outlining every male muscle in his powerful thighs and buttocks. As he slid into the base, the umpire thrust his arms out to his sides. The reaction of her father and three brothers was to whoop and holler and slap each other in masculine camaraderie.

It was then that her father saw her.

"Baby." He jumped up and took her into his arms in a fierce hug. "You look tired, honey." He guided her to the thickly cushioned sofa of soft pastels piped in a lime green. Libby found herself inanely wondering for the hundredth time how her mother, a woman of impeccable taste and breeding, could allow her furniture to be abused with such male disregard as she spied the uncoastered cold beer bottles atop the antique cherry tea table, sweating little beads of water over the matte finish.

Her brothers each jumped up, affectionately welcoming her with their pet nicknames and getting in a teasing remark.

Her oldest brother, Charles, skimmed his knuckle down her nose. "How goes the life of fighting for truth and justice? Did you render any criminals helpless by the sweep of your lashes or by tying them up with your pantyhose?" He laid an enthusiastic kiss on her forehead.

"Actually…" Libby sank down gratefully into a thick-cushioned easy chair as her mother handed her a crystal goblet of Chablis. "You may hear about my last assignment over national news during the next few days."

"Oh?" Libby's mother looked worried as she perched herself gracefully on a high wingback Edwardian chair.

Libby brought her glass to her lips, pleased that she had gotten their attention as she watched her brothers settle their gazes on her. Even her father waited expectantly. But then the taste of the wine got her own attention. She gingerly placed the glass on the sideboard, thinking better of it. She would stick with iced tea until she knew.

Libby's mother clutched her own glass delicately. "Tell us about it, dear," she asked politely, although Libby knew the last thing her mother wanted to hear was anything involving her daughter and danger.

"Actually, it started out as a drug smugg—"

"What?" Her mother let out a horrified gasp.

With a loud roar from the TV, all the male heads turned in unison and their eyes fixed on the screen. Her youngest brother, Nicholas, leaped off the couch and started shouting obscenities at one of the players while her father waved his hand in disgust before taking a long deep swallow of his beer.

After several minutes of debating the play, they finally turned their attention back to her.

"Never mind." She sighed. "Sabotaging the largest sex ring in the country is nothing—"

"Sex?" her other brother, Wade, piped up, momentarily interested. "Tell us about it over dinner," he beamed before turning back to the TV.

Libby's mother shrugged and then pulled her up to lead her away. "Come and see my latest find."

Libby was awed as she entered the den and studied the small marbled smoking table and ran her fingertips along the cool stone. She guessed its date somewhere in the early 1820's. "It's lovely, Mother."

"I knew you'd appreciate it. I so wish you still lived here. We'd have such fun at the auctions. This was from an old estate on the northeast side of Central Park."

Libby admired the blue hue of the old marble. "Well, I promise I'll be back for the symphony, Mother. I know Daddy will be thrilled to give up his ticket to me."

The faint trill of a bell signaled dinner, but before Libby responded to its call, her mother laid a restraining hand on her shoulder. The fine lines around her wide-set brown eyes deepened. "Your father's news is about his new store opening in Tyson's Corner next year."

Libby's heart leaped in anticipation. "So, the Board approved it? That's just fifteen minutes from where I live." Her enthusiasm paled as she saw the thread of sympathy in her mother's expression and awareness dawned. "And you're telling me now so that when Daddy announces it, I don't do what I just did with you, which is to assume I'll be working there in some meaningful capacity."

Her mother's eyes softened. "I don't know why you'd even want to work for your father, dear. He would be no different with you. You know he believes that soon you'll give up all your career aspirations in favor of marriage and children, no matter how many times you insist that won't happen or that you wouldn't let those things interfere with your goals."

Any protest Libby could muster died with the last of her mother's words. After these last few days of worry, she knew everything would change if there was a baby coming. She was amazed that she had always blindly refused to see it, too quick to criticize women who changed their career tracks with impending motherhood.

Libby simply nodded in acknowledgment, stunned by the irony of her timing. At this point she had far more pressing concerns than her career. And the store was a long way from being complete.

"Don't worry, Mother." She squeezed her mother's hand. "I'll let Daddy make his announcement and I'll hold my tongue."

Her mother rewarded her with a grateful smile.

"But this is far from over," Libby added. "I'll still fight for my rightful place in this family."

"In the business," her mother corrected. "Never forget that, sweetheart." Her mother stroked her hand. "There's a difference. Actually, Libby, I don't know why you've never considered approaching Nordstrom's at Tyson's Corner."

"Daddy's fiercest competitor?"

Her mother answered with a small smile.

\* \* \* \* \*

When the subway stopped at Brooklyn's 4th and Brody station, Michael took the steps two at a time and finally emerged onto the cement sidewalk, his back pooling with sweat. Before he headed two blocks east to his mother's small house in Brooklyn, he tapped the pack of Marlboros against his palm and lit up. Then he stopped at the Italian deli for some cannolis.

The smell of the spaghetti and meatballs reached him before he cleared the top stoop of his childhood home. His mother swung the screen door open to greet him, wiping her hands fastidiously on her faded apron.

"Perfect timing." She smiled as he wrapped her in a bear hug for which she promptly scolded him, claiming he was crushing her bones. "Your brother just got home from work, too." She insisted he wipe his feet even though there hadn't been a drop of rain in days. As he stepped into the small duplex, the smells of wood polish and room freshener competed with the spicy sauce, creating the nostalgic welcoming that never changed. His mother and this house remained the only constants in his life.

"Tell your brother to turn off that TV and come eat." His mother waved him into the small kitchen.

The Braves and Phillies game was in its seventh inning. Michael had been following it on the train on his way up and knew his brother, Brian, would fill him in on what he missed.

When Michael walked into the small living room with its threadbare braided rug, they shook hands and studied the TV as they talked. "What's the score?"

"Oh, man, you just missed it. Chipper Jones was called out on strike and Bobby Cox is going wild over the call." Brian laughed. "It was beautiful."

"Boys?" their mother called. "Meatballs are on the table."

"Okay, Ma, this inning's almost over."

It was an old trick and one she always fell for. A few minutes later she was placing their plates on the long coffee table as they argued over each pitch and then predicted the final score. They both agreed about how the season would shake down.

After the tension of the last weeks, and especially the last few days trying to forget Libby, Michael was grateful for the diversion. But then, like a jinx, an alluring vision of Libby sprang to mind that he found hard to smother.

He grabbed for his cigarettes, offering his brother one from the pack.

"You smoking again?" Brian asked in surprise.

"Yeah."

"More meatballs, honey?" His mother waved a ladle at him and set down the ceramic bowl.

Michael smiled indulgently. "Are you sure you're not half Italian, Mom? I'm full. Save them for another night."

She patted his cheek. "I'll wait on dessert until Maggie gets here." She trudged back to the kitchen.

The meatballs settled like lead in his stomach. Another image, this time of a small curvaceous brunette with eager eyes, flashed before him. He groaned. He couldn't see her. Not when this thing with Libby was still unsettled. He rubbed his hand hard along the worn slipcovers and frowned.

He nudged Brian. "Did Maggie call?"

His brother eyed him impatiently. "You should have told her you were coming this weekend. You know how good she is about keeping up with Mom while you're gone. It embarrassed her that I assumed she knew."

"This three day hiatus came up unexpectedly. I didn't think to call her."

His brother gave him a chafing look. "Exactly."

"What does that mean?"

"You tell me." Brian sighed. "Just tell me one thing. Have you slept with her?"

"That's not something—"

"I have a reason for asking." Brian slapped down his beer. "If you're not interested enough to see her then I'm going to ask her out, but if you've already slept—"

"I haven't."

Brian hesitated. "So, I've got the go ahead?"

"Yeah. I'll talk to her tonight."

* * * * *

Michael needn't have worried about letting Maggie down easy. She seemed to have expected it.

She looked so young as she gazed at him questioningly. "Is there someone else?"

"Not exactly, no," he answered her honestly.

"But your hoping there will be?"

"Not really. It's a little complicated."

"Michael, *you're* complicated." She shifted uneasily and glanced away. "And a little overwhelming."

He sighed. "I'm sorry, Maggie."

Later that weekend, as he replaced some rotting boards on his mother's porch and then fiddled with the air-conditioner, he thought of his youngest brother with Maggie. His ex-wife had dumped him a year ago, and everyone but Brian saw it coming. While marrying a New York City firefighter was a novelty for his upper-east side wife at first, her upbringing hardly prepared her for the lifestyle of the working class. The adventure soured after just two years, and his divorce was now in its final stages.

Maggie would be good for Brian. She was from the neighborhood, and her father was retired from the utility company. Brian would be a step up for her, although Michael doubted she thought of it in that way.

His other brother, Danny, hadn't faired any better than Brian. When Danny stopped by to cut the grass, he told Michael that he was taking his ex-wife back to court for the third time to prevent her from moving his twin girls across the country—another consequence of her recent promotion. Michael closed his mind to his mother's stricken look when she had overheard the news.

Michael bore down and watched the power drill twist the last screw out of its socket and thought about his brother Matthew's disastrous shotgun marriage and how hard it was on his parents to be restricted in seeing their only grandchild, Sean. When Danny's twins were born it eased the pain. But then within the last year his father had died, and now his mother would be suffering again over more grandchildren she didn't get to see.

For being raised in a good Catholic home, the Mulcahy boys weren't doing too well.

Without warning, the imagined scent of Libby's hair filled his senses, so vivid in its remembrance—an expensive tang of perfume and honey, a rich luxuriant aroma that flooded him along with images of the feel of the silken strands sifting through his fingers and the smooth warmth of her thighs against his. His cock swelled in his Levis.

"Damn it…" He yanked the cover off the air-conditioner. As he checked for frayed wires he shoved aside all renegade thoughts, refusing to allow himself to think about her. It only fueled his frustration and reminded him of his carelessness the last time he had made love to her. He didn't know why the thought kept nagging at him. He dug into his breast pocket for a cigarette. She didn't seem worried. If she was, she would have said so. Why should he waste sleep over it?

* * * * *

Libby alighted from the cab as it pulled up before Grand Central Station and lugged her overnight bag off the seat beside her. She let it rest on the sidewalk a minute before dragging it the never-ending distance to track fourteen. It was stupid not to bring her suitcase with wheels, but she had thought it too large for just three days. She should have agreed to let her brother accompany her to the train when he'd insisted.

She heaved the strap onto her shoulder. Because the leather dug into her skin through the thin fabric of her dress, she ended up dragging rather than lifting. Hoisting it one more time off the pavement, she tottered through the thick double doors and into the main lobby as she looked about for attendants. But this wasn't the airport. People were used to carrying their own bags. Finally, she got lucky and spotted a young man a distance away just as she felt the weight miraculously lift off her aching shoulder. She turned and bumped into a wall of chest. She didn't have to look up to know who it was. She would know that clean male scent anywhere.

A blur of soft leather indicated he had thrown her bag up easily onto his massive shoulder.

She looked blandly into those clear blue eyes fringed with dark lashes and for a moment her heart slammed into her breast. Two trains, and she *had* to pick the one he'd be on.

"I'm handling it, Mulcahy." She grabbed at the strap and motioned to the skycap who was now nowhere in sight.

"I got it," he drawled.

"You don't have to." She wrenched on it but he didn't budge.

His frown deepened and his gaze penetrated hers. "It's too heavy for you to lift."

"Ever been told you're a male chauvinist?"

"Many times," he replied dryly, turning her solidly in the direction of their gate.

She shrugged lightly, dismissing his comment. "You are insufferable, Mulcahy."

"Insufferable," he muttered with a shake of his head.

She scurried ahead of him, leaving him to struggle with both bags, although he didn't seem to be struggling at all, but instead gained on her in seconds, cupping her elbow protectively and guiding her to the escalator.

She shrugged out of his hold. "I can find my way."

He grunted behind her as she stepped onto the moving top of the stairs. His hand rested on her hip. She sighed silently. It was an unconscious gesture on his part, yet one that sent her pulse quickening. His protectiveness was so automatic that she felt almost foolish objecting, but they weren't a couple. He had made that clear. In fact, they were a mistake.

"Would you mind removing your hand?"

He glanced down and frowned, slipping his hand off her with a bored shrug.

The terminal was filling up with weekend commuters catching the last trains running between the Washington/Boston Corridor and filing in from the surrounding suburbs. Libby recognized the Wall Street executives arriving from Long Island, soon to give up their tennis rackets and Dockers for briefcases and three-piece suits, while their wives remained at summer homes in the Hamptons, their children at camp. Libby had been one of those children, and although she loved her summers at the ocean she couldn't picture herself being that kind of a mother.

When she stepped off at the bottom of the escalator, Michael grabbed her from behind, his thick arm whipping around her waist and pulling her against him as a small cart of cleaning supplies whizzed by, the worker who pushed it at a brisk pace oblivious to the merging crowds.

The solid feel of him reminded her of those nights sleeping with him, tucked up into his warmth, his breath caressing her neck. The sweet memory of it tugged at her heart.

"Watch yourself," he murmured in her ear.

"I've been at train terminals before."

"You wouldn't know it."

"How do you think I managed up until now?"

He snorted. "Over this way," he mumbled, guiding her around a throng of people at a magazine stand, his large palm resting possessively on the small of her back and the weight of it seeping sensual warmth down through her limbs. But it wasn't his fault. His touching her was unconscious, one he would explain as natural. She smirked; his response was that of a dominant male with what he considered the weaker half of the species.

Her thoughts skipped to his "Donna Reed" at home, wondering whether he had seen her this weekend. Her heart reflexively tightened at the notion.

"Sit here." He set her down in the last spot left on the wide maple bench. Neon signs overhead blinked that their train had arrived, its departure expected on schedule. He settled the suitcases at his feet and stood before her, arms folded over his chest, his stance wide, as though guarding her.

She tossed him an annoyed glance, shifting on her seat. His eyes dropped to her legs. She tugged at her hem, but his gaze remained riveted on her calves and then traveled up her legs as though trying to peek under her skirt, further fueling her annoyance, but she could tell he was unaware of his blatant ogling. He ran a hand through his hair and sighed before glancing away.

The loudspeaker blared that Amtrak number fourteen was now boarding, the neon flashing in a rapid stutter. Michael reached down and touched her elbow.

"I can manage," she clipped, jumping up and starting for the stairs. After all, *he* was the one carrying the bags.

He snickered behind her.

The line bottlenecked for a moment and she whirled on him. "If you have something to say, say it."

He lifted a brow.

"Well?"

Nothing. He just stared, his eyes half-lidded and amused. Why did she let him goad her? Up this close, the rough shadow of his beard seemed darker.

As soon as they stepped in, she grabbed for her bag, intending to take the single seat to the left, not trusting herself to sit next to him for almost three hours.

He moved the bag out of her reach.

"Would you give that to me?" When she yanked on it, he dropped it with a thud at her feet.

"Take it." He turned abruptly to the two empty seats to the right.

She dragged the bag across to her seat and settled it beside her. From the corner of her eye she saw Mulcahy take the seat across the aisle. She unzipped the side pouch of her bag and lifted out the small paperback her mother had given her, written by one of her favorite romance authors, Susan Elizabeth Phillips. For the first time Libby read the title and smiled ironically. *Nobody's Baby but Mine.* Poor timing. But her mother must have sensed her mood, because she told Libby she had laughed aloud while reading it and was sure Libby would too.

She placed it face down on her lap so that Michael, sitting diagonally across the aisle, wouldn't see it, and she tucked her bag beside her.

"You'll have to put that overheard, Miss," the conductor said as he cruised up the aisle checking tickets. Libby showed him her pass and faked a clutch at the handle until he passed while other passengers obediently threw their bags in compartments over their seats. She looked up to see Michael snap shut the large storage place above him. She had pushed her bag far enough under her seat so that it was partially out of sight, and she draped her legs over it.

The murmur of voices settled as people flipped up briefcases and snapped open papers. The older man beside her reclined back his seat and shut off his reading light. Her stomach lurched as the scent of his sweet cologne reached her nostrils, the scent too strong. Lord, that's all she'd need now was to vomit. She froze with the realization that she felt nauseous but then quickly dismissed it as an overreaction.

"You can't keep that there, Miss." The conductor pointed to her oversized bag. Before she could protest, he turned to the two women across from her and punched their tickets, but then he turned back to eye her impatiently. With an irritated sigh, she lugged the bag onto her seat and rested it while she propped open the cubicle. The hinges caught and held.

She glanced around. The conductor was a few rows back, but he gave her a subtle signal that he was watching.

She tried to heave the bag up to her shoulder first. A wasted effort. Stuffed as it was with shoes, books, a blow dryer, curling iron, various containers of lotions, moisturizers and creams, it was like a dead weight.

The man beside her began a light snore.

She made another valiant attempt to lift the bag onto her shoulder, not knowing what she'd do once she got it there. She didn't have to worry; her arm gave way, sending the bag tumbling into the center aisle.

Michael was reclined, his long legs stretched into the aisle and his arms folded over his chest. "Need any help?" His lips twitched and his blue eyes glittered with amusement.

She brushed her hair off her forehead and glared at him. It was so unfair. He took his male strength for granted. How lucky to be spared the helplessness that for woman invariably surfaced at the worst times.

He eased himself up and with one hand tossed her bag overhead as though it were a lunch sack, then he snapped the hinges shut. He peered down at her as she stood sandwiched between him and the arm of her seat, his breath warm on her forehead.

"Thank you." Her words slipped out on a breath.

His eyes softened and his gaze dropped to her lips and then up again. "You're welcome," he said, his lips curling at one corner and then he stepped back, allowing her to return to her seat.

As she dropped back down to settle into her seat the train lights shut off and a few hands reached up to snap on the small intensity lamps. She could feel his eyes on her. When she finally mustered the courage to glance his way, he was resting back, his eyes closed.

His closeness for that brief moment had unsettled her and then drawn her to him like a magnet.

Her cubicle grew stuffy with that annoying cologne and now stale cigarettes as the young woman across from her draped her jacket over her knees and extended her legs. The smells mixing with the plastic of the worn vinyl seats made her squeamish.

She peeked at Michael. His lips were relaxed. She thought of how he smelled. Since he was obviously asleep, maybe she'd go sit in the empty seat beside him. Just until her nausea subsided.

Her eyes traveled across his broad torso and then over long, work-roughened fingers that were lightly entwined over his belt. She lingered on his narrow hips and then the defined bulge in his Levis. The soft, faded denim hugged his thighs and skimmed along the contours of his long legs. She fidgeted in her seat and tried to ignore the smells as she propped open her novel. She'd wait until she was sure he was asleep.

* * * * *

Michael smiled to himself as he felt Libby settle in beside him while he continued to pretend sleep. She had waited at least a half hour before crossing that aisle. He felt her seat recline and sensed her rest along his body just short of touching him. He feigned enough sleepy restlessness to turn so the full length of his leg pressed along hers. She leaned her head on his shoulder, making it natural for him to settle his lips into her hair. Her warm honey scent welcomed him.

He missed this. Missed sleeping with her. Maybe she did, too.

To his surprise, he felt himself relax and drift off to sleep.

# Chapter Nine

"Rewind the tape," Stephen howled for the third time as the small team gathered in his office to wrap up the sex resort investigation. He drew the blinds tighter and flipped off the light. While Libby had been pointing out the members of the group that they suspected as decoys for further follow-up, the team was busy ogling all the naked women from that last recorded session, right before the agency had busted in. Even Morgan showed surprising interest, particularly when the young couple got into it on the carpet. Libby felt herself flush with embarrassment as the male agents watched in rapt attention the young man take the woman from behind.

"We shouldn't be watching this," she murmured.

Not one person responded or even appeared as though they'd heard her.

Then to her dismay they finally allowed the tape to continue only to stop it again and rewind when the big guy Libby was partnered with slipped his hand up her skirt. The sight of Mulcahy storming across the room and pouncing on the guy had them riveted. She groaned when they rewound it to watch again.

Libby herself watched Michael's fury in awe as he grabbed the guy up by his collar, and her stomach fluttered at hearing him call her his wife.

Morgan smirked. "You were certainly convincing, Michael."

Stephen smiled. "Yeah, good show you put on. What would you have done if the team hadn't stormed in? Pummel the guy into the carpet?"

Mulcahy simply grunted, his cheeks hollowing as he drew a deep drag on his cigarette. Stephen poured vodka and tonic into glasses and offered them around. It was after hours and these impromptu meetings often took the edge off an intense day.

When Libby politely refused the liquor, Mulcahy shot her a sharp glance. While she had done her best to avoid him since their train incident, occasionally she found herself having to face him and with it the memories of their nights together. She shifted uncomfortably in her seat. She should know that it didn't take much to arouse suspicion in an FBI agent.

Stephen's brow arched. "Just a little, maybe?"

She waved him away but then reconsidered. "Just give me the tonic and lime, thank you."

Mulcahy's eyes were now burning a hole in her throat. She could feel the delicate pulse at the base of her neck jump as she crossed her legs gracefully and accepted the virgin drink.

Even Morgan seemed to study her with curiosity. She felt like a lush who had suddenly gone on the wagon. Then she watched her friend's hand flutter discreetly to her mouth. Libby groaned privately. It wasn't easy being surrounded by a roomful of agents. Morgan was too bright not to know that Libby was keeping something from her, particularly since Libby hadn't wanted to discuss their assignment even though Morgan teased her endlessly, dying to know. Libby belatedly regretted that she hadn't told Morgan. And she wondered why. Isn't that what women did? Especially at a time like this when she really needed a friend?

As the session ended, she went to catch up with Morgan, but she found her in conference with Steven, his concentration intense. Libby waited a moment but then decided they were engrossed in a conversation that was not likely to end soon. She'd talk to her tomorrow.

As she lifted her linen jacket off the corner hook and slid her weary arms into the three-quarter length sleeves she could feel him behind her. It was as though the heat from Mulcahy's body radiated out to touch her in the most intimate way. She drew in a breath, reluctant to face him.

His silent question had weighed heavily between them since they'd returned. He would not rest until she gave him a definitive no on the results of their "unprotected sex." As though the scientific plausibility demanded it. She stifled a sigh. How could she sense so much about a man that she barely knew? While most men would have been glad to dismiss the possibility, he apparently had to be in control. And now she had raised a red flag by refusing the alcohol. Why did the man have to be so intense?

When she finally turned to him, she couldn't help but think that he gave the impression of a man whose energy was barely contained in his powerful body.

"Libby?" He lifted a tentative hand as if to touch her and then caught himself. He dropped his hand by his side. "I know I'm overbearing sometimes."

"Sometimes?" Her automatic response caused her a moment of guilt because his gaze was sincere.

"Most of the time," he grudgingly admitted.

She felt her defenses begin to melt and a small part of her wanted to comfort him. She gave a little sigh. If she was right about him, she had some idea what he was going through.

All week she had studied her body for impending signs, but she had hardly known what to look for. And she was afraid to search the Internet for information as though it would bring bad luck. She stifled a small smile at the thought that thinking about being pregnant could make it so. As he stood before her now, her mind tumbled back to that long night of lovemaking.

"Libby?" His eyes were deep pools of blue. For a moment she had an odd impulse to rest her head against a shoulder that looked as steady as solid rock. "I just want to make sure—"

Stephen interrupted them with a call for Michael from his brother. He waved Stephen away, but Libby insisted he take the call. He argued with her but she cut him off and placed the phone in his hand. When he finally took it, she could see the deep lines of concern etched across his forehead. Although he turned aside, she couldn't help but hear him murmur reassurances into the phone. From what she overheard, he would be heading right back to New York by the end of the week.

Knowing the call would take awhile, she excused herself. He nodded.

* * * * *

The awful wait was made easier for Libby after she confided in Morgan. While at first her friend was stunned, she later insisted that she should have guessed. To Libby's astonishment, Morgan now believed Mulcahy had avoided her from the start because he found himself attracted to a woman who was his obvious polar opposite and he was scared witless. Libby had laughed at her assessment. Michael Mulcahy wasn't afraid of anything—least of all, her.

She waited through the days necessary before she could administer the home pregnancy test; she chided herself for wallowing in self-pity. She was twenty-eight and should have known better. She shuddered to think of the impossible struggles other less fortunate women faced. She doubted she'd be strong under different circumstances.

When the five days had finally passed and she could administer the test, she reminded herself before dipping the test stick under her stream of urine that the instructions claimed it might take several long minutes for results to appear. Blue for pregnant, no change for not pregnant. If the strip turned only a faint blue, for better accuracy, the purchaser should let a week pass and then repeat the test.

Her strip turned navy within seconds.

Any remnants of hope disappeared with the toss of the strip into the wastebasket. She couldn't believe it. One time, just that once, and she was pregnant. She perched on the edge of the tub, her heart hammering in her chest. She was no longer dealing in theory—this was real. And while another woman's circumstances would offer her *some* options, Libby knew her privileged status offered her only one. This child could not be denied her heritage.

Then there was Michael. Would he expect her to have an abortion? Somehow she doubted that as much as she doubted that he'd simply fade into the background, allowing her to raise this child her way, his only responsibility that of signing a monthly support check—

support that she didn't need. The entanglements of her life multiplied with each passing moment.

It was a terrifying thought—the possibility of being connected to such a domineering male. There would be no partnership, he would simply take over.

Ironically, that realization brought her a moment of calm. For, once his true character firmly rooted in her heart, it would be just a matter of time before he would cease to attract her. This thing with him was simply physical and it would pass.

* * * * *

Upon arriving at work on Monday, she discovered he had stayed in New York. She was relieved to find he would be gone all week, affording her much needed time alone with her news. She would use this week's respite from him to plan how to approach him.

But then she learned the reason for his extended stay. Over the weekend his mother had suffered a mild stroke. How could she present him with more to deal with?

When the following Monday arrived, despite the long week, her heart was in her throat. His cold disregard for her the morning after their infamous night together came back to stir up emotions she had effectively repressed. He had said what they did was a mistake. She glanced at the clock. Six. In just one hour he would know the exact extent of that mistake.

Knowing he would be staying late in his office to catch up on missed work, she waited until the floor cleared. But when she approached his door, no light shone under the threshold. Her immediate response was relief. Then she admonished herself for her cowardice and stifled a low moan, knowing she had to do this.

She gave a few light taps and then entered tentatively, peeking her head around the door. The room was bathed in the golden shadows of dusk, the filtered shades fully drawn and blocking out harsh light. He was sitting in the middle of his sofa, his head resting over the back with his legs sprawled out before him. Papers pooled at his feet and a portfolio rested on his lap.

When he looked up with a start she knew he had been dozing. His eyes had that half-lidded sleepy look she remembered well from so many mornings. Her eyes dropped down his chest, skittered away, and then rested safely on the bulk of his forearms. His sleeves were rolled back, the mat of dark hair stark against the white cotton. He tossed the portfolio aside and then sat up, anxiously clenching his hands. With the effort, muscles rippled from his wrist to his elbow. She blinked and drew her gaze back to his face.

He ran a weary hand through his hair. For a moment she felt guilty for her intrusion until she reminded herself of the appalling nature of her interruption. It would represent more than a moment's interruption in his life. Yet, her impeccable manners still prompted her to apologize.

"I'm sorry to interrupt," she said with her practiced air of self-composure. When she thought of the warmth with which she responded to him just three weeks ago, she almost cried for that woman that she was. No logic held her emotions in check that night, and memories of her passion with him came flooding back to taunt her.

He nodded, motioning for her to sit. But the massive set to his shoulders was so intimidating that she felt safer standing. He perched on the couch's edge, his legs spread wide and hands resting between them. She wondered inanely how men could be so casual in the way they practically cupped their sex when they sat before a women. One would think having three brothers would render her immune to such male ways, but it didn't.

The air bristled with tension, time suspended as she stood before him mentally wringing her hands. Fine lines deepened at the corners of his eyes. He looked exhausted.

"I'm pregnant."

She simply said it. No preliminaries. All her careful planning had gone out the window after just minutes in the same room with him.

A flash of pain swept through his gaze and then he hung his head. The moment stretched as she watched those powerful shoulders droop.

With a shake of his head, he murmured, "This is all my fault." His voice was soft and his words so filled with regret they nearly dissipated in the air.

"That's hardly ever the case," she assured him. "And it certainly wasn't in ours."

"I was careless. Damn it. I haven't been that stupid since I was a teenager."

She was suddenly impatient with having this life that had been growing within her for weeks referred to as a careless, stupid mistake. "I won't have an abortion." It was important he understood that from the outset.

His head snapped up. By now she should have been used to his unpredictable responses, but again he astounded her. Catching her waist, he pulled her to him, placing the flat of his hand on her belly. "Thank you." His voice was husky with emotion. He tenderly smoothed his palm over the soft swell of her abdomen and then pressed his cheek to her. His arms came around to hold her close. She felt the rigid set of his shoulders relax.

Her breath stopped and her hand dropped spontaneously to the thick head of ebony hair nestled against her. With gentle fingers, she comforted him, sifting her fingers through his hair and gathering him to her protectively. His response was to rub the hard line of his jaw along her skirt and burrow closer. It was so unexpected, the relief she felt brought tears to her eyes.

But soon his scent reached her and replaced her more tender emotions with unbidden feelings of lust. She closed her mind against the familiar sensations, until his palm slipped under her blouse and skimmed along her midriff. "What are you doing?" she whispered.

He lifted her blouse and pressed cool lips against her heated skin. "Comforting us?" he suggested as he deftly started with her bottom buttons and then quickly worked his way up.

The war waging within her caused her reactions to slow so that in one stealth movement he had unclasped her bra and cupped her breasts. She strangled on a breath and clutched at his wrists as he laved one nipple and then the other in a manner that was more reverent than sexual. She wondered if it was his way of getting closer to the child she carried.

"They're browner," he murmured hoarsely, stroking the pads of his thumb lovingly along her sensitive tips. "And larger." He traced his index finger around the edge of her areola, skimming the line that defined where nipple met pale skin.

She relaxed her grip on his hands and patiently tried to see what he did. While her breasts had grown fuller and felt tender, she hadn't noticed this change.

"You're beautiful," he murmured. And then his light touch grew bolder. He licked her, sending sensation spiraling down, fueling the intimate ache gathering.

She half whimpered, "We shouldn't do this." Her fingers tangled in his hair when she meant to push him away, feeling his tongue hot on her.

"We need each other now," he mumbled, his lips tracing a path down her midriff while both his hands slid up her skirt.

"Michael, no." His searching fingers skimmed across the lace of her bottom. "We can't do this." She grabbed at his hands, now buried under her skirt.

"You're right." He dropped his arms and then ran his hands down his face. "Remind me why we can't?"

She clutched her blouse closed, sputtering on a response that wouldn't come.

He tipped his head. "You can't get any more pregnant." He blinked innocently.

Her mouth gaped. In a matter of minutes he had her head spinning. She willed herself to gain composure. Someone had to exercise some common sense. "We're not a couple, Michael. We're merely two people…caught in a situation in which we'll have to learn to work together."

His eyes were tracing up her legs. She pulled instinctively at her hem, trying without success to reach her knees. Finally she gave up, and with a sigh of impatience made an effort to straighten herself, quickly buttoning her blouse over her bare breasts.

"This is too new for you to fully absorb," she commented sensibly. "I've had a week to think about it. I suggest we get together in a few days, whenever you're ready."

Oddly, his lips curved in response and he leaned back into the couch, pure male satisfaction gracing his stubborn face. She realized then that he was gazing at her breasts, tight against the sheer silk of her blouse. She didn't have to look to know what he saw — she could feel it. Her nipples were hardened to points and tingling mercilessly. The memory of his teeth grazing along her that one and only night they made love rose up to feed the restless ache now consuming her as silk slid against bare skin. She wanted to throttle him.

"Instead of ogling my breasts you should be thinking of some appropriate response."

He sat up and frowned.

"Do you *have* any response?"

"You don't want to know it."

"Yes, I do," she assured him. "Tell me what comes to mind. We can evaluate it later."

His eyes glittered. He rose deliberately and walked toward her as he spoke. "What comes to mind is that I want to lay you out on that couch where I can strip you naked, kiss every inch of your flesh, and then bury myself inside you."

Her heart tripped over itself and then picked up to a roaring pace. She stepped back from him. "What does that have to do with our problem?"

"Nothing." The rough edge to his voice sent heat spiking through her. "You wanted me to give you some response."

She lost track of his words, too aware of him stepping closer. Her senses were heightened by the smell of his skin. She closed her eyes, trying to keep her thoughts on track but all she could think of was the hard feel of him laying on top of her. "Open your eyes," he commanded her gently.

They snapped wide.

"I want you, Libby." He tipped her chin up and pressed his lips to hers, gentle at first and then hard and demanding. She felt herself going limp in his arms but he held her up easily. She didn't understand how she could respond so quickly to him. As though reading her thoughts, he tangled his tongue with hers, stroking suggestively, teasing her, withdrawing one minute, coaxing her the next to open her mouth and seek him. Then he plunged into the depths of her mouth, claiming her.

She sparked to life, grabbing onto his shoulders shamelessly and sucking gently on his tongue in an intimate response. She reached up on her toes to wrap her arms around his neck. He growled deep in his throat and pressed the full length of her against him. She moaned at the evidence of his arousal.

"Jesus, I want you," he groaned. He slid restlessly against her, pulling sensation from every inch of her. He lifted her effortlessly and brought her to the couch.

The next few moments were a blur as he pulled his shirttails out of his belt and yanked off his shirt impatiently. She studied the light mat of dark fur covering him and watched his rippling biceps as he stripped off every bit of clothing and stood before her fully aroused, the thick purpled head of his erection glistening and angry-looking. She squirmed as he descended toward her, every vital, flexing pound of him.

With a grace that belied the sheer size of him, he plucked off each scrap of lace and silk with a flourish until he got to her panties. He made stripping her an art as he licked around the elastic edges and tangled his tongue in the lace overlaying the silk. Then he ripped them off with a vengeance and spread her wider.

She squeaked when he reared back to get a good look, separating her swollen lips with his fingers. "God, you are so fuckable."

His crude language only further aroused her. And then he licked hungrily between her legs, swirling his tongue around her clit until she was clutching at his hair. Her body dissolved into a liquid puddle of pleasure as he sucked and licked until every nerve was heightened to a frenzy. "You're delicious," he growled. "Christ, I'll never get enough of you."

When he drew her clit between his lips and suckled hard, she cried out, pounding on him to stop.

"No more," she gasped. "I can't." Her words got swallowed on a strangled sigh when he plunged two thick fingers into her, taking her swiftly over the edge. She was drowning in sheer bliss, her body swimming in an ecstasy of sensation. She sobbed out his name and then burst into tears.

When he pulled himself up along her body, he entered her with an urgency that frightened her at first, so fierce was his need, and then he drove her up again into a dizzying heat, the burning tension of pleasure even more satisfying for the feel of him filling her.

"Libby," he groaned, driving into her hard. "I'll never get enough of you." He thrust over and over again, hitching deeper and straining for her, buried to his root, until she tightened to an unbearable pitch, writhing restlessly under him and then exploding. He grew unbelievably hard and then his release burst through her, the warm liquid soothing the friction created by their joined bodies. She held him close, his muscled body achingly helpless in her arms. She wanted him to stay inside her like this forever.

The thought froze in her brain, her awareness heightening to a red alert. She could feel his heart pounding against her breast, and the wiry mat of hair covering his body still tingled her flesh. He ran his hand down the length of her, skimming her hip and thigh as he eased off her.

"You're so smooth." He pressed his lips to her stomach and lingered before crawling up her body and resting his head on her shoulder. He lay with his other arm wrapped around her waist, pressing her to him.

"My God, what did we do?" she breathed.

He moaned into her neck. "Don't make me talk now. Please, I just can't do it."

No, he couldn't. Nor did she believe they would ever be able to carry on a rational conversation. Yet, in minutes he'd had her completely in his power. It was as though she had no will of her own.

"I can't handle this," she said, struggling to sit and letting him drop onto the couch beside her. As soon as she slipped off the couch and bent to gather up pieces of her clothing, he gripped her ankle.

"Where are you going?" He pulled her back.

"I can't stay here." She tried to escape but they fought a tug-of-war for her ankle.

"Libby," he said, his voice soft and pleading, but still holding her ankle in a death grip. "Stay."

She turned to him, clutching the small bundle of clothing in her lap, her leg twisting and pulling at his wrist. "Let me go."

He slipped onto the floor and crawled toward her. She could read the concern in his eyes; still, she didn't trust herself to stay another minute. He finally let her shake off his hold. In crab-like fashion she inched away from him along the plush carpet.

He blinked his baby blues. "Don't go. You said we needed to talk, remember?" He prowled around her like a supple animal in a slow graceful rhythm, muscles flexing and rippling.

She scoffed. "There is little chance of that ever happening and you know it."

As though to confirm it, he slid his hand idly up her calf. But she knew he was hardly aware of what he was doing. She was convinced that for him touching her was as natural as breathing.

"See?" She yanked her leg away and scrambled to her knees, the small bundle of clothes that she clutched her only cover.

He half sprawled alongside her and touched her knee. "Okay." He closed his eyes. "What do you want me to say?"

For one naïve moment she thought he was joking, but then she realized he was serious. This would be worse than she thought, but she was too exhausted and fraught with anxiety to know where to begin.

"This can't continue." She shoved her arms into her blouse and buttoned it, fully conscious of his gaze following her every move. Then she stood and slipped into her skirt. She gave up on her underwear while her eyes searched for her shoes. They were across the room, beside her bra.

He murmured, clutching at her skirt, "Don't run away." The plea evident in his deep voice went straight to her heart. Still, she yanked out of his grip and ran across the room.

He hopped alongside her, slipping his legs into his shorts and trying to grab her at the same time.

"This is how you got us into this in the first place," she clipped, snatching up one shoe while searching for the other.

He stumbled after her. "Me? You agreed—"

"With your scientific theories and mating patterns," she said, snapping up her bra just as she spotted her lost shoe.

"Look, I'm sorry—"

She scraped up her last shoe and delivered one final jab. "Perhaps you could design our dilemma into a working hypothesis that we could test out, experientially. We'll collect data and analyze our results."

He kneaded his forehead and sighed.

She took her window of opportunity and raced for the door. He beat her to it and leaned his heavy bulk against the doorjamb. He crossed his arms.

She grabbed for the doorknob anyway, but he pressed his hand against an oak panel. She tugged with both hands—a wasted effort.

"Are you going to let me leave?" She blasted him with a scathing look.

"No."

"Why not?"

"Because we're in the middle of a fight."

"Let me out of here. I can't be near you. We've got enough complications as it is."

He sighed. "Libby."

"Let me go."

He scowled. "Fine. Go." He yanked open the door.

As soon as she escaped from him, she heard it slam behind her.

# Chapter Ten

Saturday evening the humidity was oppressive. Michael cursed himself for not taking a cab when the sweat trickled down his back. He could afford a cab now, but taking the subway was force of habit. He grimaced. The Upper East Side of New York City was more than an expensive cab fare from Brooklyn; it was a world away.

He glanced at the small sheet between his fingers as he turned west on Lexington. On the paper a tiny rose raised the surface of one corner—he swore it smelled of her. Libby's feminine script was stark against the lavender color that penned the number of her parents' penthouse. It would be on the south end of Central Park.

The entrance was an imposing marble and stone courtyard with large potted plants lining the brick walkway under the green striped awnings. He buried his cigarette in one of the pots as a uniformed doorman asked his name and consulted a guest list before letting Michael through the thick brass doors. As he slid up through sixteen floors, he checked his hair in the chrome trim. It was getting a little long for Bureau standards. He ran his hand carelessly through the top. Nothing he could do about it now. Although Libby had insisted he dress casually, he hoped his khakis and polo were all right. Christ, why was he worried? It was August in the city. Not a time to be walking around in a suit.

When he and Libby had attempted to talk the week following their—in her words—"unrestrained physical contact," she had insisted on a hands-off policy. She claimed that though it was true they were to be parents together, they were "horribly mismatched" in addition to knowing nothing about each other—other than their knowledge in a biblical sense. He smiled to himself; they were definitely acquainted there.

Still, he acknowledged a nod of guilt in the way he took such pleasure in her resistance, in the way he had to work for her. She claimed it was amusing that he was so easily aroused by her, but he knew it made her nervous. *He* found his continual arousal around her natural.

He granted that things did have to be decided, a plan set in motion. Since twenty percent of pregnancies end in miscarriage, when she suggested they wait through her first trimester to tell their families, he agreed. But he suggested they meet now so when they broke the news in a couple of months it would be less shocking. Libby had concurred. That's when she pointed out that they were only pretending to be dating. The hands-off policy was necessary to avoid any further complications. He didn't understand how things could *get* any more complicated. But he had reluctantly agreed; he didn't have much choice.

When he stopped before the thick paneled door numbered Suite 1601, he took a deep breath before knocking. In minutes the door swung open and Libby stood before him in a pale silky dress that clung to the delicate shape of her body. The sight of her always hit him like an electric bolt and then the heaviness settled in his groin. A heaviness that wouldn't subside while she was near. It was as though every nerve was strung tight and waiting for relief.

As he stood silently drinking in the sight of her, he realized she hadn't said a word. He smiled tentatively. "May I come in?"

She swallowed lightly and stepped aside to allow him to enter.

In a reflex as natural as breathing, he circled her waist and held their hips tight to each other. He ducked down, settling his lips over hers, swallowing her startled gasp with his tongue for a quick taste. She was sweet and delicious.

He shifted his erection to settle between the soft curves of her thighs. He sighed in satisfaction. A perfect fit.

"Michael." She gasped against his lips. "We agreed."

He chuckled softly. "It'd look funny if I shook your hand."

"A peck on the cheek would do."

"Not in my family."

"Well this is *my* family."

He released her abruptly. "For crying out loud," he mumbled.

In a breathless sweep, her eyes dropped to his bulge and then up to his face again.

"It's only natural, Libby." He smiled at her stricken expression.

She turned on sandaled high heels and those gorgeous long legs, tossed her honeyed hair at him, and clipped off. It took considerable willpower to resist smacking her adorable backside. Jesus, he wanted to devour her. Instead, as he followed after her, he contented himself with watching her hips swaying under her short skirt and fantasized that she wore no panties. Fat chance.

Reality drifted back as she escorted him into a large sunken living room filled with the kind of antiques he saw only in magazines and the elite hotels the Bureau put him up in occasionally.

Like her daughter, Libby's mother was the model of etiquette as she extended her hand to welcome him. Yet she hesitated for a bare fraction of a second as she regarded him with well-concealed curiosity that only a FBI agent of fifteen years would detect.

"Mrs. Vandermark, it's a pleasure." Michael took her hand and nodded.

"Please, call me Meredith." Her smile was warm but reserved.

Another nod from Michael and she was motioning him to a plush cushioned couch across from the chair in which she descended gracefully, crossing her low-heeled shoes at the ankles. He was amused to see Libby hesitate before she sat down beside him, and even then she was careful that their bodies didn't actually touch. Her mother's gaze flickered politely between them before she spoke. He got the feeling that this woman didn't miss much.

"May I get you something to drink?"

About to answer, he stopped when Libby and her mother turned to the sound of a burly voice and the slam of a door. Michael felt the quiet atmosphere churn as though a storm approached when the dark-haired man, shorter than him but stocky, bounded down the few carpeted steps to join them. The butler trailed after him, catching up first his suit jacket and then his tie as the man carelessly dropped them anyplace convenient. His smile was wide as he approached Libby's mother and Michael got the impression he'd scoop her into his arms if she'd let him, but the amused warning in her eyes subtly held him at bay. He pressed her cheek lightly in greeting before turning to Libby.

"There's my baby girl," his voice boomed as he took hold of her shoulders and gave her a firm kiss on her forehead. "You're looking pale. Are you okay?"

Libby gave him a rueful smile. "I'm always pale, Daddy."

But Michael knew her morning nausea all this week hadn't helped.

"Daddy, this is Michael Mulcahy."

Her father's easy manner tempered subtly as he narrowed steel gray eyes at Michael. "Mulcahy." He nodded, capturing Michael's hand in an iron grip and giving him a quick once over. Michael found himself straightening his shoulders and meeting him eye to eye. A shrewd gleam caught in the older man's expression as he studied Michael a moment. Michael doubted much got past this man, either. Then a flash of recognition softened his gaze.

He released his hand and pointed a finger at Michael. "Quarterback, Penn State, 1990. Am I right?"

Michael gave a quick nod, a grin edging his lips. "Yes, sir."

His brows arched. "You still follow the game?"

Michael responded with surprise. "Of course."

Her father chuckled. "Well, I'll be damned." He shook his head and then winked at his wife when she placed a restraining hand on his arm. Michael smiled to himself. He was sure the message was for her husband to watch his language. Michael felt an immediate affinity for Libby's old man, and the affection between her parents was unmistakable, if discreet.

"What can I get you to drink, son?" Libby's father motioned to the butler who stood at attention off to the side.

"A beer would be fine, sir," Michael replied.

The old man smiled and nodded as the man he called Rahoul whisked off and then returned with two bottles of Coors, a fresh glass of white wine for Mrs. Vandermark, and an iced tea for Libby.

Throughout dinner Libby's father kept him on the hot seat, firing one question after another in between a meal of baked salmon that rivaled that of the best restaurants in Washington D.C.

Michael was surprised to learn that Libby's father never finished high school and that the Vandermark name represented nothing before her father's success except a fancy sound. He'd worked hard in the oil fields in Texas, saved more than he spent, and got lucky with a little piece of ground that held more oil than dirt. Michael guessed that luck was only part of his success. The man exuded a confidence and vitality that was hard to miss.

He smiled at his wife.

"I was a young upstart when I met Libby's mother. Thought I had the world by the tail 'til she came out with her daddy, who was looking to buy stock in my oil refineries when my company went public. Oil prices were going crazy then. I hardly knew which direction to go 'til he took me under his wing and gave me a little guidance. It wasn't his attention I wanted, though. I thought Meredith was the prettiest thing I'd ever seen. I was newly rich and had my pick of girls, but she wouldn't give me the time of day."

Meredith gave him an indulgent smile, her impeccable manners probably preventing her from responding more openly. This was such a contrast to the way his own parents had been with each other. His father, a robust Irishman, had always grabbed up his mother at the wrong times. And like a young girl, his mother would laugh and tease him further. Yet Michael doubted Libby's parents loved each other any less.

Bill Vandermark tossed down his linen napkin with a flourish and tilted his chair back. "What about your parents, Michael?"

"My father died last year, sir. He was a New York City detective most of his life until he retired after thirty-five years. He was one year into retirement when he had a massive coronary. He went quick and quiet, but my mother's having a hard time."

Libby's mother's eyes filled with sympathy while her father placed his beer bottle down with a thud. "Damned shame. Man works hard all his life and then doesn't get to enjoy his later years. Sorry to hear that, son. Your mother live here in the city?"

Michael told them about his family in Brooklyn and he had no choice but to mention his brothers' divorces since questions about grandchildren cropped up. He and Libby would be going to his brother Danny's house tomorrow.

And then the shrewd older man raised the question they'd both been dreading. "I thought the Bureau had policies on agents getting involved?"

Michael gave a cautious glance to Libby, who spoke up quickly. "They do, Daddy. Michael and I are keeping this under wraps for a couple of months and then, if necessary, one of us will quit."

Her father frowned. He was probably wondering why Libby bothered to introduce him at all if she wasn't sure he'd be around in two months.

Her parents exchanged quizzical glances.

Bill Vandermark's eyes pierced Michael's. "What happens if you're found out?"

Libby squirmed in her seat. "It won't come to that, Daddy. One of us will quit before anyone suspects…if we need to."

"I see." Her father nodded reasonably but Michael knew he didn't understand at all and wondered again how he and Libby thought they could pull this off. He was bound to raise suspicion himself tomorrow with his own family.

"Well…" Mr. Vandermark pushed away from the table. "What say we wait a bit on dessert, Meredith. Michael and I will have some whiskey in my den, give us a chance to get to know each other."

"Fine, dear. I'd like to show Libby the rosewood Marquetry table I found."

Libby gave Michael an anxious look but followed after her mother.

After the older couple exchanged knowing glances, Bill led Michael down a wide hall and into a richly paneled den, replete with heavy maple and leather furniture. The air was thick with tension. He felt as if he were facing a firing squad.

As soon as Michael was settled on a couch, whiskey in hand, Bill got right to the point.

"What's going on, son?"

"Sir?"

Vandermark leaned against a large stone fireplace, lightly twirling the fat squat rocks glass in his hand while he studied Michael quietly. "My daughter's as nervous around you as a nun in a whore house. Every time you look at her, I think she's going to leap out of the chair."

Michael groaned inwardly and then slumped back into the chair.

"Is she pregnant?"

Michael's head shot up. Damn, the old man was perceptive. *What a way to meet his future in-laws.* His brain froze on that flashing thought, and time lay suspended as he tried to sort out where it came from. But he had no time to analyze it. Libby's father waited for an answer.

"Yes, sir." Michael straightened, fully expecting a burst of rage and he was prepared to take full responsibility. "It's all my fault."

To his surprise, Bill Vandermark snorted. "It's rarely one person's fault."

"I seduced her, sir." Way to go, Mulcahy. Why not get him *good* and mad. The trouble was, it was the truth.

"I don't doubt that. What I can't figure is how you succeeded." Vandermark shook his head. "My daughter goes out of her way to avoid men like you." He downed a long gulp of whiskey and winced.

"Yes, sir." Michael gulped a swallow of his own. "But we were on assignment together…in close quarters."

Vandermark paced before the mantle and then stopped. "When were you going to tell us?"

"When we were sure everything was all right."

"She's not at any risk?"

"No. But she's only four weeks pregnant." The thought of her carrying his baby sliced through him. It was impossible for him to think of it in theoretical terms, pregnancy just didn't convey the import of what was happening.

Libby's father nodded thoughtfully and then shook his head. "And with that job of hers? FBI agent?" He snorted. "But she doesn't listen to me."

"I'm looking after her, sir. I'll make sure she's not given any assignments that might jeopardize her condition."

"What happens in two months?"

Michael wanted to assure him that he would do right by Libby and marry her and to his surprise the idea felt right to him, too. But she would be furious with him for suggesting it to her father when they hadn't even discussed it themselves. "We haven't gotten that far."

Vandermark looked at him sharply. "You'll marry her, though?" Michael didn't think it was a question and looking at the formidable man he could see as himself years from now if he were to find his own daughter in this situation. Suddenly he knew it was the only honorable solution. But could he convince Libby?

"I don't know that she'll have me, sir."

The older man's impressive shoulders sagged with relief but his expression turned troubled. "Yes...Libby," he murmured as he dropped himself onto the couch to sit beside Michael. Both men grew silent and stared at the rough stone of the dormant fireplace. Bill grinned wryly. "You know she got a perfect verbal score on the SATs?" He shook his head. "Damned hard to win an argument with her." Before Michael could respond, the door quietly opened and Libby walked in to join them.

"Dessert is ready," she informed them with an air of polite caution.

Michael didn't know whether it was the look of guilt on his face or her father's brows drawn together in worry that alerted her, but Libby was too clever not to know something had passed between the two men.

Her father jumped up. "Baby." He kissed her forehead solicitously.

That clinched it. She wrestled out of her father's grasp and whirled on Michael. "You told him?" Her voice was incredulous as she stalked over to him, fists clenched and her body vibrating with rage.

She was shaking before him, daring him to deny it, but all he could think was how beautiful her flushed skin looked and how her eyes sparkled with life. He took both her hands in his in an attempt to get her to sit beside him. He needed to reassure her that he hadn't betrayed her. "Libb—"

"We agreed," she railed at him, tugging on her wrists.

"Your father guessed, Libby," Michael said quietly.

"Let go of me." She pried at his wrists but he held her firmly.

"Listen—"

Her father interceded. "He's right, baby. He had no choice but to tell me everything."

Her scathing eyes darted from her father back to Michael. "Everything?" A bright blush stained her cheeks.

Her father touched her shoulder. "Don't blame him, honey—"

She whirled on her father. "You're defending him?" she choked.

Michael released his grip and sank back into the sofa, thankful to be momentarily off the hook.

"Baby—"

"I see," she clipped. "Of course, you would. No doubt you've *both* wrapped this little predicament up nice and neat and are now prepared to explain to me what will happen next."

Her father looked perplexed.

"Am I right, Daddy?"

"Well, Michael agrees you should marry him—"

"What?"

Michael looked at her gaping mouth and broke into a sweat. He sunk lower into the couch.

"Is that what you two have been doing in here? Planning my life for me?" She looked with indignation from one to the other. "I suppose you've already decided that I'm the one who should quit my job?"

"Well, yes," her father responded with surprise. "But Michael said he'll make sure you're not given any dangerous assignments until then."

Michael dropped his head into his hands and groaned.

While Libby sputtered something nonsensical, Michael looked up to see her mother poised in the doorway. It didn't take Mrs. Vandermark long to assess the situation and float magically in and sweep her husband away. "Come, Bill." She clutched his arm, and to Michael's surprise, he obediently followed her out of the room.

With the soft close of the door, the room fell into blessed silence but the air still crackled with tension.

Libby stood rigid, looking shell-shocked, her hands locked before her in a grip so tight her knuckles were white. Her soft lush mouth was pinched with frustration. He wanted to gather her into his arms and kiss her into bliss, but somehow, he didn't think she'd appreciate it. Yet, he was too drawn to her to remain seated and instinctively rose.

She looked over, startled for an instant as he moved closer, her gaze in a fog of confusion that quickly moved into focus with his approaching steps and then filled with anxiety. It occurred to him that, despite their polar personalities, this was one thing they shared. She didn't trust herself with him, physically, and he couldn't keep himself away from her.

"Libby." He clutched at her waist, but she jumped away from him.

"Don't touch me."

He held his palms up, at least succeeding in getting her to stop backing away. "I'm sorry," he said softly. "Your father is a shrewd man. And he has his own way of deciding things and thinking it's settled."

She gave a ladylike snort and brushed her fingers through her hair in a gesture that was entirely female. He could see her body soften and it took every ounce of willpower to keep from catching her up.

She sighed and then sank down into a padded wingback chair, clutching its arm with one hand, her vulnerability so arousingly feminine that he was drawn to her like a magnet. He watched as she ran her slim fingers through the ends of her hair and stared ahead, troubled and enticingly soft.

"I'll just drown," she murmured more to herself than to him.

He wanted to touch her, comfort her, but the last thing she needed now was for him to confuse things by turning this physical and, ultimately, sexual.

She turned imploring eyes to him. "So then, you didn't tell my father you'd keep me off dangerous assignments?"

In an automatic gesture, he glanced away before answering. She astutely read his response for what it was and snatched the opportunity to interrogate him.

"Then you must have also told my father you'd marry me?" Her horrified expression suddenly irritated him. Didn't she realize it was one option they should consider? It gave their child legitimacy.

"Of course I said I'd marry you," he scowled, wondering belatedly how he got himself into admitting that.

"Without having discussed it with me?"

The appalled lilt to her words infuriated him. "Your father asked me. What was I to say? It's the only honorable thing to do."

She leaped off the couch. "I don't believe this. It's another time warp. Don't I have any say in this?" Her eyes blazed at him.

"Of course you get to say something." He kneaded his temple. The conversation was getting away from him. "I mean—"

"That's generous of you." She whirled on him and ran toward the door.

"Oh no, you don't." He raced after her and snatched her up easily, turning her around to face him. She pounded against his chest but he pulled her wrists above her head and flattened the backs of her hands against the door. Before she could kick him, he locked her feet between his own and pressed his weight, effectively pinning her to the door. "You're not going anywhere." He had her trapped, hip to hip.

"Let me go."

"No." Her lips were a breath away but he couldn't let himself get distracted, they needed to have this out. But then he groaned as he felt his involuntary response to his hips pressed against her soft curves. She smelled so...Libby—delicious.

His mouth was on her, soft but insistent. She bucked against him, twisting and pulling, refusing to give him an inch as his hands held her firmly. But this was stupid. He couldn't keep doing this. Maybe she was right and it was his way of avoiding talking things out, he thought as he continued to press her warm lips and feel the heat and curves of her body against his. But just as he eased up, he felt her melt into him, soft and yielding, her body surrendering to his as a small, strangled sigh escaped her lips. He probed with his tongue and she opened to him, her taste warm and wet and delicious.

"Ah, Libby," he whispered. She collapsed in his arms. He held her close, his tongue swirling and stroking hers. *He could handle a lifetime of this.*

"This doesn't solve anything," she said on a sound caught between a moan and a sigh.

"But it feels better than fighting."

She released a tiny sob as he nibbled at her neck. "What about Donna Reed at home waiting for you? The woman who is willing to quit her job, stay at home, and raise the five kids."

"Four."

"Whatever."

He traced his thumb along her full lower lip. "I ended it." He kissed her gently. "I couldn't go out with one woman while lusting after another."

She suddenly stiffened under his touch. "Were you sleeping with her when you seduced me?"

If she was trying to hide her vulnerability with that question she hadn't succeeded. There was so much about her that surprised him, like some unfathomable mystery unfurling at every turn.

"No. How could I?"

"I see." She pressed her forehead against his chest and let out a deep sigh. Cradling her was as natural as breathing.

"Can we hold off any discussions for now? We've got my family to face tomorrow."

"I'll agree to the 'no talking rule' if you'll agree to the 'hands-off' one.'"

"Libby, it's not natural for me."

She pushed gently away. "Look, Mr. Science. It isn't natural for me to avoid talking. Do we have a deal?"

He massaged the back of his neck. How did he get himself backed into agreeing on this again?

"You know we're horribly mismatched and you said yourself we don't even like each—"

"Okay," he barked, shoving his hand into his hair and stepping away. "No talking and no touching. Agreed?"

She nodded.

He shot out his hand to seal the truce but she snatched hers away. "No touching of any kind."

With the speed of light he grabbed her up and kissed her, pressing the full length of his body to hers. He chuckled at her stricken expression. Before releasing her, he licked her lips.

"Starting now." He smiled and then stepped back.

She gave him a haughty reprimand before sailing out the door.

\* \* \* \* \*

They didn't fare much better the next day in Bergen County, North Jersey, for the barbeque at his brother's house. His mother was polite but puzzled. And although Michael tried to chalk it up to the mild stroke she had recently suffered, he knew she was in full command of her faculties.

His brothers each dragged him aside at first opportunity, and Michael was irritated when they implied a similarity between Libby and Brian's spoiled ex-wife from Central Park West. Of course, it didn't help that further conversation brought out that Libby had attended Brian's wife's Cotillion Ball when they were both young debutantes.

Michael didn't see the comparison, although at one point he did. While he had been sure it would be a mistake to get involved with Libby for all those reasons, he was seeing things differently now. Libby worked as hard as anyone in the Bureau and Michael now saw her as quiet and reserved rather than the aloof ice maiden he had once thought her. Still, his brothers questioned his wisdom in wandering so far afield from his roots.

While Michael no longer thought of his making love to Libby as a mistake, he decided that *this* event was a disaster. The only redeeming value was watching Libby with his twin nieces. She allowed them to brush her hair endlessly, clipping up and tying the long loose strands with fancy bows and ribbons. They marveled over her polished nails and to the girls' delight, after getting their father's permission, Libby painted each of their nails from a small supply in her bag. Michael was amazed at how much one woman could carry in her purse.

And it didn't matter that her attempts to play ball with Sean had her missing every other catch and throwing wild, because his young nephew had obviously developed a huge crush on her before the day ended.

By the time they left for the train that evening to take them back to Washington, she was exhausted, yet still she refused to let him cradle her against his shoulder in the cab and at the train track. He was surprised she let him carry her bag. Her fierce independence irritated him. In some ways it wouldn't be easy raising a child with her. But he shook off the thought before it sank deeper, knowing he had to concentrate on her positive qualities, of which there were plenty.

His gaze traveled involuntarily along her bare legs, drawing to memory their satiny feel.

# Chapter Eleven

Libby didn't know how she would survive another meeting in the same room with Michael and prayed they would not be put on assignment together. Although during this last month he had adhered to their little truce in practice, he blatantly disregarded it in spirit. He didn't have to touch her for her to feel him. It was as though they defied the laws of physics, and she knew he felt it too. She laughed at her scientific assessment. But then a panic attack struck, thinking of next month and the decisions they would have to make.

She took a deep breath before she pushed open Dr. Clark's office door and joined her colleagues in the comfortable circle of chairs.

Michael relaxed back, his tilted chair rocking beside the director. When she saw Stephen and Morgan settled on his other side she was thankful to be spared sitting next to him. Other chairs were taken up by a couple of forensic specialists and a DNA expert.

Libby was the last to seat herself and while she greeted everyone and received their acknowledgement, Michael simply traced his eyes down her legs. She knew he didn't intend to be so blatant. If she asked, he'd probably claim it just came naturally, but she worried that someone was bound to notice. Her mind flashed back to their meeting months ago in Stephen's office when he did the same thing as she sat across from him at the conference table. At the time, she thought he was being purposely intimidating. How differently she perceived things now.

Still, the fact that she was convinced he harbored no hostility toward her, and never had, didn't make it easier. He had never once suggested that he liked her, only that he had a strong physical attraction to her.

She felt tears well up before she could stop them, once again so frustrated with her emotionality these last weeks. She blamed it on the pregnancy but she knew that it was only half responsible. If she didn't get control of herself, she'd find him leaping out of his chair to go to her, and hadn't they raised enough suspicions already? She was sure Stephen and Dr. Clark guessed there was something between them. Morgan had come to her rescue more than once to throw off the scent.

Michael was far too protective of her to claim just a casual relationship and for the hundredth time she wondered why he wasn't concerned about Dr. Clark finding out.

"Are you familiar with our guy, Libby?"

The director's voice brought her out of her malaise and she was appalled to realize she had no idea what criminal they were referring to. She looked about; they were all staring at her and waiting.

Michael frowned and dropped his chair back on all fours. She had better focus before he drew her aside and insisted on taking her home to rest or questioned her about what she ate for lunch. For a man who was uncommunicative, he was very perceptive and as much as his domineering ways frightened her, they also offered some comfort. He might not love her, but she believed he'd never let anything happen to her in her vulnerable pregnant state.

She rallied quickly. "I'm sorry, Dr. Clark."

"Rainie Vigiano...the tortoise. Slow but sure." The director gave a half smile. "Morgan will fill you in on the financial fraud end of it and forensics is prepared to go over all the physical evidence connecting him with places and key people. Stephen has your identity all ready. The problem, Libby," he continued, scratching his jaw, "is that everything we have is circumstantial. We need a confession, an admission of his involvement in the activities."

Dread seeped through every pore. She was afraid where this was leading. When she glanced involuntarily at Michael, he was watching the director closely and looked ready to pounce.

"How do I fit into this?" she asked quietly. She spoke without a trace of the anxiety she felt, her cool unruffled manner so integral to her nature that she wondered if her passion with Michael was simply an aberration, never to resurface, and if she would eventually bury all emotion to the point of extinguishing it forever.

She reproached herself for her philosophical ruminations and forced herself to pay attention.

Stephen filled in for the director. "The man's sly, been alluding us for years. But through a former girlfriend, who has turned federal witness, we've discovered his one flaw. He has a weakness for beautiful women and can't resist a little boastful pillow talk."

Morgan handed her an 8x10 glossy photo of a tall sandy-haired man with an impressive tan and a billboard smile. She had expected someone Italian from the underworld to look dark and sinister but this man resembled more a well-dressed celebrity than a dangerous criminal. A tall voluptuous redhead in a low-cut red sequined gown draped his arm.

Surely, Libby was not expected to attract his attention. The Bureau must have arranged a way for them to meet.

"Michael, you'll head up a team to watch over Libby."

When she handed the photo back to Stephen she asked, "How will I meet him?"

Stephen glanced at Dr. Clark and they both smiled. "I don't think you'll need to worry about that. He'll find you. We'll plant you at one of the casinos."

Libby was perplexed. "And you expect him to notice me?"

All the men turned and looked at her blankly.

"Of course," Dr. Clark replied.

"Why, that could take weeks, if ever," Libby explained. "Surely you can come up with something more efficient."

"Any artificial meeting might draw suspicion," Stephen said. "Believe me, it'll be effective."

Libby didn't see how, but she quickly dismissed it for now, because when she looked up, Michael was perched on the edge of his chair, his brows drawn sharply together and his eyes glittering.

"It's too dangerous," he snapped. "She's not going to do it."

The group turned in unison and stared.

"Put someone else on it. Libby's not available for this one."

Stephen guffawed. "Since when? Who made you guardian angel?"

"Back off, Stephen."

"Besides," Stephen continued, "this guy's not dangerous with women. No history of violence there. Apparently, he likes them wet and willing."

Michael glared at him.

"Sorry," Stephen said, turning quickly to Morgan and Libby. "I meant *warm* and willing." The other men chuckled while Stephen went on to explain how it would go down. "You'll have to tap his bedroom at first opportunity, Libby, and we'll supply you with enough tranquillizers to safely knock him out before he can get too intimate, but not before his tongue gets a little loose. And since you have the skill to get information out of a block of cement, this should be easy. He'll wake up in the morning hoping he was a wild stud but not able to remember a thing. It'll be up to you to reassure him." Stephen laughed.

Libby groaned inwardly and suddenly felt ready to retch. "Excuse me." She rose sedately from her chair and walked calmly out.

"We could all use a break," the director commented as she headed out the door.

Safe in the ladies room, she dabbed her heated skin with cool water. She wanted to believe it was just her morning nausea but the thought of another covert assignment brought her to the edges of panic. Why did she put herself through this? It never had and never would convince her father of anything.

After a long calming moment, she forced herself out into the hall only to be met by a body of steel.

Michael clamped his arm around her waist and drew her over to a deserted alcove. It did no good to resist him. He was simply too powerful for her…and too stubborn.

"What is it?" she asked with an impatient clip.

"You're not taking this assignment."

She scoffed. "Why?"

"You heard Stephen. The guy's been involved in underworld operations for years."

"I *am* an FBI agent," she drawled. "There's no immediate danger. I won't be wearing a wire or carrying a gun. I'll be fishing for information and you'll be close by if things get stirred up."

"That's not the point," he scowled.

"Then what is?"

He dragged a hand through his hair and paced. "Damn it, Libby," he barked. "You're preg—" He stopped and looked around and then drew her farther into the alcove. He leaned in above her. "You're going to have a baby. I'm worried." In a moment of tenderness, he traced a finger along her chin. She might have listened if he had finished his objection with an expression of concern for her as well, but when he didn't, she removed his hand.

"I'll be lounging by the pools all day and watching the gamblers in the evenings. How stressful can that be? After I meet him, I imagine I'll spend the rest of my time in bed."

He reared above her. "You will not."

She raised a cool brow at the same time that her heart begged him to say what she wanted to hear.

"I'm responsible for you." His obligated expression made her heart sink.

"For the baby," she retorted, the words catching in her throat as the vision of a blue-eyed boy with dark curls sprang before her. "You're responsible for the baby, not me." She lifted her chin and tried to shove her way past him. "I can take care of myself."

He gripped her shoulders. "No, you can't. And I won't let you take this assignment."

His high-handedness was so blatantly chauvinistic that for more than a moment she was stunned into silence, but only for a moment before she came back at him. "You're *telling* me I'm not taking this assignment?"

"Yes." He ground out the word.

If she expected him to back down like a rational person, she was wrong. She sighed. "Did anyone ever tell you that you were born in the wrong century?" She smoothed a hand through her hair. "Now let me go. They're probably waiting for us."

He appeared on the edge of total frustration, his massive shoulders bunched thick with tension and his handsome face in a deep scowl. Then she saw it in his eyes, that look he got just before he grabbed her up and devoured her.

She held up a restraining hand. "It's not going to work. You have no claim on me. And just because you can effectively melt all my defenses *temporarily* doesn't mean I've given in to you, so don't bother using physical force to get your way."

"Force?"

She glanced away. "Persuasion then."

"Michael, Libby, we're ready to start."

*Saved by the bell.*

It was Libby's last thought as they followed Morgan back into the briefing room.

* * * * *

That night, Libby shifted restlessly, drawing her knees up tight to her chest and awakening just enough to toss herself on her other side and drift off into sleep again. She winced and bit her lip the next time she awoke, but this time she stayed awake and listened to the heavy sound of her breathing and felt her nightshirt stick to her skin. A cramp seized her and stripped away the last fog of sleep as her focus sharpened on the sensation. Menstrual cramps. Only she wasn't having her period and these were stronger. She waited. It came again, fierce and strong, making her double up in pain.

As soon as it subsided, she fumbled the phone out of its cradle and punched in the familiar sequence of numbers, relieved when Morgan answered on the first ring. Her clock flashed four a.m. Only a fellow agent would respond with such speed.

By the time Morgan arrived, the first stains spotted the sheets. As Morgan helped her slip into jeans while they waited for the cab, a small gush of blood soaked the pad she wore. And by the time they arrived in the emergency room, Libby was drenched in blood and crying amidst the terminology bouncing about.

"Eight weeks, BP ninety over fifty. We should probably do a CBC."

"Do you know where you are, Ms. Vandermark?"

"The hospital," Libby murmured, while dizziness overtook her and then a sharp pain as her arm was flattened and tape was smoothed over her skin. Her brain registered the IV just before she drifted off, barely feeling her heels being anchored in the stir-ups.

She didn't know how much later it was that her mental fog lifted, allowing her to hear voices murmuring about kids' tennis lessons, the cost of hockey equipment and then nothing again — darkness — until the voices finally grew louder. But this time she recognized a voice, one voice, Morgan. Her lids fluttered open to see her friend standing quietly beside her, the lights dimmed, other voices hushed, a few moans. And then another voice as she closed her eyes again.

"Wake up, Ms. Vandermark." An annoying pat on her hand.

*Let me sleep*.

"Come on now. Wake up."

Libby moaned. Morgan gazed down at her. "You okay?" She gave Libby a worried smile.

"Where am I?"

"Recovery room. The doctor will be in."

Libby groaned, her eyes unsuccessfully following the brightly clad figure whose quick movements blurred around her.

Before long her vitals were checked and pronounced satisfactory. The doctor explained they hadn't done a D&C because she had ejected a placenta and an empty sac and then her cervix efficiently closed on its own. Probably an incomplete fertilization, no pathology, she assured Libby and suggested that she could wait a few months and try again. For now, she advised Libby to take a few days off from work and rest. Libby had lost a fair amount of blood, but other than that she was in perfect health. No worries.

Libby burst into tears. Hormones, the doctor assured her, that will probably make her a little crazy for a bit until they settle back to their non-pregnant state.

After the doctor left, Morgan helped her dress and then got them a cab that safely deposited them back at Libby's small apartment in Bethesda. Morgan said she'd stay for as long as Libby needed her. Libby nodded numbly, too drained to respond.

Once settled onto the couch, embroidered pillows propped around the overstuffed loveseat, the two women sat opposite each other cradling hot cups of tea. It finally sank in. Libby was no longer pregnant. Maybe never had been, truly. She had fallen in love with a concept, imagined a possibility, but rather than feel relieved, she felt empty.

Morgan handed her a piece of honey-wheat berry toast from a delicate blue Wedgwood plate. "When are you going to call Michael?"

Libby ran her finger along the smooth edge of the bone china and leaned deeper into the couch, avoiding Morgan's question.

"This lets you both off the hook, doesn't it?" her friend asked, her voice soft and cautious.

Tears, unexpected and uncontrollable, welled up. Libby choked on a sob.

"Oh, Libby."

"It's just the hormones." Libby waved her hand dismissively. "And as soon as they settle, I'll tell him."

"You can't wait until then, Libby."

"Why not?" Her voice was a silent plea.

Morgan's only answer was a sympathetic tilt of her head.

Libby sighed. "I'll...I'll call him tonight." She placed her cup gingerly on the dark teak coffee table. "But Morgan, you don't understand what he's like."

Morgan frowned. "I have some idea."

"He's complicated."

"I'll bet." She smiled. "Are you in love with him?"

The question took her by surprise. And although her first instinct was to deny it, what would be the point? Instead, she responded, "I hardly know him. Besides, he's very domineering, Morgan." She paused. "I don't mean in a work situation. He's an excellent agent. But in a personal situation..." She shook her head. "He's overwhelming."

# Chapter Twelve

Libby's little nap later that morning turned into an entire day's sleep, but she felt rested when she awoke.

As she padded across to her bathroom, her grandmother's old wedding clock chimed seven, its solid gold chains swinging and glittering as the early evening sun of late summer speared through the slated blinds.

She was famished, but first she hopped into the shower to let the soothing beat of her shower massager awaken her further. When she brushed her teeth and scrubbed her face with the lightly pitted apricot scrub, her stubborn sleepy haze lifted and the events of this morning came flooding back.

For a while she had succeeded in relegating them to the back of her mind, but now her sense of well being faded as a nagging worry surfaced. What if everything wasn't all right?

After she dried her body, she patted her hair with a small towel and stepped naked into the air-conditioned chill of her bedroom.

The large frame of Mulcahy loomed before her, halting her on a stunned gasp. She wrapped the towel ineffectively around her. "What are you doing here? How did you get past the doorman?"

"And you call yourself an FBI agent?" He gave her an amused frown, making no attempt to look away. "Damn, it's nice we keep meeting like this, Libby." He reached for her in a gesture that seemed as natural as breathing.

She jumped back. "Stay right there." What made him think he could grab her up at will? She stifled a sigh of envy at his confidence.

He ignored her. His eyes grew heavy-lidded and he kept coming until he backed her against the wall. He leaned in close, flattening his hands against the wall, trapping her. "You smell good," he breathed.

Next he would press his erection against her and it would be all over. But even warning herself did no good. The thought of him holding her, filling her, flooded her with warmth and a need she could hardly stand.

Before she could duck under his arm he caught her nipple in his lips and slipped his hand between her legs. She moaned when he brushed her clit lightly with his thumb and slid a long finger through her sex. "You're always wet for me, Libby," he murmured.

She pushed on his shoulders in a weak protest just as his other hand reached around to cup her bottom. The feel of his calloused fingertips skimming along her buttocks was torture. She'd never resist him if she didn't stop this now. "Michael," she cried just as he slipped two fingers up between her folds. She tightened with pain, still raw from all she'd been through.

When she struggled for him to release her, he gave an annoyed grunt but finally let her go. As she grabbed her robe off the closet hook, she could feel his eyes on her bottom. She threw it over her shoulders and tucked it around her.

She ignored him, picking her brush off her dresser instead and heading out to the living room. "Why are you here, Michael?" When she glanced back, he was taking in the contents of her bedroom. She thought about what he saw. The eyelet curtains, the lacy coverlet and abundance of fluffy pillows with shams in coordinating colors on her queen-size bed. The tiny white bear at its center.

"Mulcahy," she snapped.

He turned, a pleased grin on his face.

She raised a brow. "Amusing yourself?"

His answering smile was tender. "I like it." He glanced around the living room. Same ultra feminine décor, complete with delicate china cups holding fresh rose petals on the end tables.

"Reminds me of when I would sneak into the girl's dorm at Penn State. It was like entering another world." He smiled appreciatively. "A lone male among all that feminine stuff," he murmured, his voice trailing off.

That he is, she thought, as he dropped his hard body down onto the plush lavender couch and moved the pillow from his back to give himself more room. He settled the frilly square on his thighs. His hair and skin were dark against the pastel colors and his five o'clock shadow was stark at this hour. He was oddly out of place and yet he looked right at home as he swung his ankle atop his knee and relaxed back.

"I was worried about you. You didn't answer your phone all afternoon or your buzzer just now." He glanced down at the pillow on his lap, smoothing it awkwardly, and then noticed the blood on his hand.

She wanted to die. Before she could read his expression, she jumped up and ran into the bathroom for some pads. He was after her in a flash, pounding on the bathroom door. "Libby, open up, damn it. Are you all right? What's happened?"

"Go away," she railed at him, knowing he wouldn't and knowing she had no right to demand it, but she couldn't face him, face everything that had happened and what it meant for them both. She just wanted to rest and forget things for a while.

"Don't make me break down this door."

She collapsed onto the edge of the tub and sobbed.

He must have heard it. "Libby, I'm sorry, just let me in."

"Last night...I had a miscarriage," she choked, loud enough for him to hear.

"Ah, Jesus." The doorknob rattled. She heard the doorframe crack as he pushed open the door. Before she knew what was happening, he was lifting her into his arms. She clung to him, burying her face in his shirt and crying tears she couldn't seem to stop.

He descended into the easy chair in the corner and just held her, running his fingers through her hair and rocking her gently. "Shh..." he crooned, his deep voice low and soothing. Without her fully realizing what he was doing, he took the thick pad that she still clutched between her fingers and opened her robe. He lifted her gently and placed it between her legs. She was too upset to be mortified.

She didn't know how long she allowed herself the luxury of his protective embrace, but she couldn't stay like this forever, although a part of her, more than a part, longed to.

After a time, she made herself sit up. She wiped her tears with the back of her hand. She had to stop this ceaseless crying. She insisted to him that she felt better and finally straightened in his arms. "Would you make us some tea?" she asked, needing time to compose herself before she faced him.

While he heated water, she slipped on a pair of panties and washed her tear-stained face. When she finally joined him in her small kitchen, seeing the look of concern on his face as he sat at the table waiting for her nearly broke her heart. She needed him now, yet she would not bind him to her, now that there was no reason to.

She dropped into the chair opposite him and circled the steaming mug with both hands. "Morgan came over and got me to the hospital. Since I was only eight weeks, it was nothing major. Actually, they assumed it was an incomplete fertilization." She hated the cold way she said it. When she glanced at him she saw his confusion. She hurried on. "I'd never heard of it, either. But apparently your sperm didn't completely penetrate my egg. When my body finally realized it..." She let her words dissolve into air.

He frowned. She wondered if he was taking exception to the accusation that his sperm didn't perform well. She would have smiled if he didn't look so distraught.

He turned his mug around in his hands. "Are you all right?"

"Yes, as you can see."

He ran a hand through his hair. "So, you're no longer pregnant."

"That's right." She thought of Morgan's comment about being off the hook. "There's no need for you to feel responsible for me anymore."

His lips parted and then formed into a hard line. He looked as though he might say something but then he glanced down at his mug and sat back. She waited, but he remained silent, staring into his tea.

"I'm sure your family will be relieved when you tell them we've broken up." She didn't expect him to answer, but she knew it was true. "Since you *told* my father I was pregnant, now I'll have to tell my parents I'm not." Before she could apologize for baiting him, his head snapped up.

"Your father guessed at the truth. What was I supposed to do? Lie?"

She waved her hand, suddenly so weary. "It doesn't matter anymore." She wanted this over before they both said things they'd regret. That she'd regret, since he was a man of few words—unless it was a science discussion. "Well, I appreciate your sense of responsibility throughout this ordeal. But your obligation to me is ended. Thank you for coming by." She rose gingerly. "I'll see you at work in a couple of days."

"I'm not leaving until I'm sure you're okay."

"Morgan is looking after me." There was no other way for him to interpret that statement other than that she didn't need him, but that was far from how she felt.

After a minute he stood with obvious reluctance and then eyed her. "Are you taking that assignment at the casinos?"

"Yes." They faced each other as though squaring off for a fight, although what she really wanted to do was surrender to his strength. The thought surprised her as much as it would him, if she ever had the courage to tell him. Of course, she wouldn't.

His jaw went rigid and a muscle ticked. What possible reason could he have for objecting now other than the one for which she hoped? She waited, giving him a chance to say what was on his mind, hoping he would tell her that he couldn't stand the thought of another man touching her, that he was falling in love with her. While her sensible inner voice scoffed at her naiveté, her heart still held hope.

His gaze was fierce as he loomed over her. But he said nothing, and she would not help him. He was the one who said they were a mistake despite that she felt they had given far more than their bodies that night, no matter how much he would deny it now.

She lifted her chin a notch.

His eyes blazed, but he didn't rise to the bait. Instead, he stormed out of the kitchen and, she feared, out of her life forever.

# Chapter Thirteen

Michael paced before the picture windows in his office as Stephen and Dr. Clark relaxed back into easy chairs watching him. It was late afternoon and both men had loosened their ties and were enjoying a scotch and soda. Libby was supposed to have returned to work today.

"Why didn't you make her give you two weeks notice?" Michael growled at the director.

"What difference would that make?" Clark exchanged an amused glance with Stephen. "Libby's between assignments and Nordstrom's wanted her as soon as possible. She was as surprised as I. Turns out her mother had sent her resume to the company. She starts immediately as the assistant to the director of marketing."

Stephen lifted his glass to Michael. "Come over here and have a drink," he cajoled him. "You should be happy. Now you don't have to look at her everyday or watch her slink up to the Tortoise, bat those big brown eyes, and slip into his bed."

Michael whirled on him. "Will you shut up?"

Stephen chuckled and twirled the ice in his drink. "Hey, what's this?" He fumbled between the cushions and held up a pair of lavender panties. He grinned and stared at the lacy garment curled over his finger.

Clark adjusted his glasses.

Michael stormed over and ripped the scrap of fabric out of his hand.

Clark cleared his throat, his frustration with Michael undisguised. "Maybe you don't know *what* you want, Michael. I thought sending you both to that spa would resolve things, but you couldn't just hang back and enjoy her. You had to uncover the largest sex ring in the country."

"Hang back?" Michael looked at his boss in astonishment. "We were on assignment, not a vacation."

Stephen and Clark exchanged glances. "A nice light one for a change," the director grunted.

Stephen smiled.

"I was busy breaking into offices, confiscating equipment."

"That's right. But if you remember, you were both instructed to just observe, see what you could piece together. I was hoping you'd make the most of your time with Libby."

"I don't believe this," Michael muttered. "I'm getting bawled out for doing my job?"

Dr. Clark ran a weary hand through his hair. "Son, I've been with the Bureau thirty years. I'm retiring this year and finally getting to spend some time with my wife. Life's too short to waste."

Stephen snorted. "I hoped it would get you off my back. You've been a pain in the ass these last six months. Nothing like a little sexual frustration to drive a man crazy."

"Look who's talking," Michael jabbed. "How long is it gonna take you to ask Morgan out?"

The director raised a brow at Stephen.

Michael left, furious with them both and furious with himself.

He had refused to think about her these last few days, and now she would be gone from his life if he let her.

He pushed through the double glass doors and squinted into the sunlight. The warm moist air pressed his lungs as he paused a minute at the top of the long cement steps leading to the courtyard below. He needed to think. He headed in the direction of the mall, an outdoor park across from the Smithsonian, and walked briskly toward the Lincoln Monument, running all his options over and over again in his mind, trying to make some sense out of his relationship with Libby — or lack of relationship — which was his fault. Although she *had* said they were "horribly mismatched." He smiled at her choice of words. Then he sobered. She was right.

A folk art festival was in full swing and colorful tapestries and indigenous acoustical music filled the air. He crossed the grassy mall, weighing the pros and cons, trying to piece together everything they had going against them and struggling to make it fit.

He took the steps to the monument two at a time, intending to find a secluded corner where he could sit awhile. When he hit the top of the stairs an idea surfaced. Then the shot rang out. Before he could turn to the sound, the pain hit and then everything turned black. The piercing pain seared straight to his heart. Then there was nothing.

\* \* \* \* \*

The hospital corridor was eerily quiet this time of night; probably as quiet as when Libby was here less than a week ago. The antiseptic smell made her queasy, but this time she couldn't blame her sensitivity to scent on her pregnancy.

Libby heard the murmur of voices coming from his room. The hospital had lifted its restriction on visitors because Michael's doctors believed he needed the stimulation to urge him out of his coma. It was his third day in intensive care. The gunshot had punctured his lung and a second shot pierced his skull where the bullet, like a ticking bomb, would remain for the rest of his life. But surgery proved a greater risk. The concussion he received when he collapsed on the stone steps further complicated his condition. The medical examiner concluded he had hit the cement corner.

His family had been there all day, every day. Thinking about the day she met them at the barbecue, Libby imagined how hard this must be. Although Michael wasn't much older than his three brothers, the entire family deferred to him. It was obvious that even his mother looked only to him in important matters. Libby remembered when her other sons were encouraging their mother to go on the senior center's scheduled cruise she had turned to Michael for advice. When he suggested she run it by her doctor, she finally agreed to look into it.

Even his nieces and nephew seemed to look to him for special approval. She understood this because his commanding presence affected everyone he met. She'd seen it in full force at work. He didn't say much, but when he did, people listened.

A host of aunts, uncles, and cousins had driven in from various states. She learned his mother was staying in a nearby hotel with his brothers who had plans to stay until Michael was out of risk and then commute from New York by train until he was released from the hospital. But the doctors hadn't actually assured anyone definitively that he would survive. The medical staff hoped for the best and were cautiously optimistic. Doctors doublespeak when confronted with their own sense of helplessness.

Michael was hooked up to a host of monitors and required a private room with 'round-the-clock care. Libby's heart ached at the thought, with a pain so deep that it left her breathless. She didn't know how she could see him without breaking down.

FBI agents were posted outside his room and at the hospital entrance. The perpetrator, who had been recently released from the state penitentiary, had been apprehended. Earlier in his career, Michael was responsible for having put the man away, and now the Bureau was taking no chances until they were sure he was working alone.

Morgan had called to let Libby know that tonight would be quiet. By the time Libby arrived at the hospital, most of the Bureau had left for the night.

She peered into his room. A myriad of wires and machines jumped and quietly beeped. She noted the tube, hooked to wall suction, protruding from his chest. They told her that his pulse was weak and thready, and the pulse ox machine by the bed, monitoring his breathing, registered an eighty-eight on the digital display. His respirations had remained shallow and his skin pale.

It worried her to see him on oxygen.

But she willed herself to be strong. The doctors had warned everyone to be careful around Michael, for many patients, after coming out of their comas, related having heard the conversations of people around them. He was surrounded now by Morgan, Stephen, Dr. Clark and Dr.

Rosenberg, an older doctor to whom she had spoken with just this morning. He was bending over Michael and speaking in a raised voice as the others looked on.

"Michael, if you can hear me, try to open your eyes. Can you hear me, Michael?"

The doctor must have gotten no reaction because he changed tactics. "Can you move your finger, Michael? Try to lift it just a little." The group waited in silence.

Libby entered quietly as they continued to hover around him. Dr. Rosenberg's forehead was creased with worry, his craggy brows knit together over the wide bridge of his nose. Libby walked up behind them and a machine beeped once and then again.

"His pulse is picking up," the doctor murmured. They all glanced at the machine overhead as jagged lines bleeped upward and settled into a pattern. It was then the doctor noticed her. He nodded and moved aside so she could approach. The machine beeped again, stuttered, and then found its rhythm. "His pulse jumped again," the doctor commented in astonishment. "I wonder if he's coming around."

Libby nodded to her colleagues and drew closer. His body, bare from the waist up, looked so strong and virile but for his paleness. This couldn't be Michael lying here. His hard-edged muscles, inert and waiting, would get impatient with this inactivity. The razor sharp line of his jaw was covered with stubble, attesting to the life within, but he remained motionless.

She skimmed her palm along his boulder-like biceps. The machine beeped again and his skin lightly pinkened. Libby snatched her hand off him in alarm and the machine slowed. The doctor looked at her keenly. "Touch him again."

Libby hesitated but Dr. Clark and the others nodded their encouragement.

She lovingly skimmed her hand along his roughened shoulder and down his arm. As the doctor must have expected, Michael's pulse picked up and his skin grew flushed.

The doctor studied her with curiosity. "Talk to him."

Libby couldn't do it. She would burst into tears and then Michael would think he was dying. She shook her head and bit back tears, as she continued to stroke along his arm and his pulse found a stronger rhythm.

"Just a few words," the doctor encouraged her.

The others waited, their eyes a silent plea. Morgan put her hand on Libby's shoulder. "Let him know you're here."

Libby drew a breath, determined to sound calm. "Michael? It's Libby." No reaction. But his heart continued to beat with the stronger rhythm.

Doctor Rosenberg motioned the others back, giving Libby more room.

She stroked him idly, the heat of his skin warming her as she slid her fingers along the inside of his forearm. She spread his palm out and languidly entwined her fingers with his. Michael's heartbeat remained at a steady pace, quicker than before but still low.

"A marked improvement," Dr. Rosenberg murmured. "If his heart rate could stay like this, it would be an encouraging sign." He read the telemetry strip. "It could have been a coincidence, but I'd like you to stay with him if you could," he said to Libby.

She nodded, her heart in her throat. *She would stay as long as it took.* She turned to the others. "I'm here now if you all want to get a bite to eat."

Dr. Clark laid a paternal hand on her shoulder and looked down at Michael. "He'll come around. He's too ornery to stay down for long."

After they left, Libby crossed the room to bring a chair over to the bed and immediately the machine beeped a warning. Before she could return to the bed, the doctor burst in and checked the wires. Libby drew up beside him. "What is it?"

"His pulse is slowing."

"Michael?" she choked, stepping back to allow the doctor to work. "I'm here. We all are." No change. She walked to the other side of the bed and laid her hand over his heart. The monitor blared and his pulse shot up.

"That's more like it." Dr. Rosenberg smiled. "I assume your relationship is special?" He raised a brow. "I mean other than being special agents."

Libby stalled with an answer.

The doctor continued. "Oh, I'm sure that isn't allowed. I'll keep it to myself. But it's important you stay with him and touch him. He does much better with you here."

The machine abruptly drew their attention. Michael's pulse spiked upward sharply, and when they glanced down at him, Libby's hand was resting on his thigh.

"Of course, if you really want to get his pulse elevated…" He gave her a teasing smile. Libby turned crimson and tactfully went back to stroking Michael's arm.

The doctor chuckled. "Well, I'll leave you alone with him. I'm on call tonight. The nurses will keep me informed of any change in his condition. Are you staying the night?"

Libby looked again at Michael. His face and chest were covered with a light sheen of sweat and his dark hair would soon be too long for Bureau standards. Small tight curls formed behind his ear and at his forehead. She couldn't see the back of his head where his shaved hair marked the location of the bullet but his dark mat of chest hair was shaved in several places where wires were affixed. She took consolation in the strong arrogant set of his jaw.

He seemed so physically powerful yet so vulnerable in his silent state. While his breathing was stronger and his skin felt warmer to the touch, she worried for him. She would ask Morgan to go to her apartment and pack a small overnight bag.

"Yes, I'm staying with him." She'd tell work it was a family crisis. And if they didn't go for it, she'd simply quit.

Dr. Rosenberg gave her a satisfied nod and left.

\* \* \* \* \*

During the night the beeping of Michael's machines woke her periodically as did the nurses who continually checked his vital signs. She slept in an easy chair next to him, placed close enough that she could rest her hand on his arm. Each time she woke to the beeping she found her hand had slipped from him. As soon as she reinstated contact, his pulse picked up. While it was still too low to be out of the danger zone, it was strong enough that the nurses no longer responded each time. They got used to waiting at their station to see if it changed back again quickly, knowing it was Libby who was the cause. One nurse had smiled and told Libby that she made their job a little easier, and as a result, the team of nurses went out of their way to make her comfortable.

Libby dreamt that night that she was making love to him, and the feelings and sensations were so vivid that she was sure she had climaxed in her sleep. It was so real, and he was so alive, his eyes dark with passion and his body vibrating with need…a need that only she could fill.

Just days ago she had vowed to make a clean break and now she found it impossible to leave him.

\* \* \* \* \*

Within days, with Libby continually at his side, Michael's condition strengthened and he floated in and out of consciousness, although he wasn't yet speaking or focusing. He would blink his eyes open and look around for short minutes, seemingly focusing on one face or object but then he'd drift off to sleep again. During one of these times he managed to squeeze his mother's hand when she spoke to him.

While at first Libby was self-conscious around his family, his mother learned the effect Libby had on her son's condition and appealed to Libby to stay by his side.

Libby couldn't help but smile at the way his brothers tried to bring him around. They accused him of faking his condition, said they got him tickets for the World Series, and generally insulted and harassed him. So much like her own brothers' tactful ways.

Libby slipped out into the hall with Morgan for a moment to leave Michael alone with his family. They hit the vending machines in the visitor's lounge. Libby was plagued with drowsiness in the afternoons that she couldn't seem to shake and she fought to keep herself alert with a candy bar.

"God, I could go for some ice cream, too. A rich vanilla...*Ben & Jerry's* Vanilla Bean," Libby said.

"We'll stop on the way home," Morgan suggested as she peeled the wrapper off her peppermint patty. "What are you going to do when he wakes up?"

Libby feigned ignorance but Morgan would not relent.

"Regardless, whether either of you acknowledge it, there is a connection between you." She eyed Libby expectantly.

Libby lost her patience. "If you'll remember, he was the one who left my apartment without a word after I told him about the miscarriage."

"You didn't exactly encourage him," Morgan accused. "Telling him he was no longer obligated."

"He wasn't. And I shouldn't *have* to encourage him," Libby retorted. "Michael Mulcahy is all male, hardly hesitant about going after what he wants." She groaned. "Did I just make that horribly sexist remark?"

Morgan chuckled but nodded agreement.

Libby took a voracious bite of chocolaty nougat and caramel and pinned her gaze on Morgan. "Anyway, he's made it very clear he doesn't want me."

"That's not what the monitors say."

Libby shrugged. "His body and his mind are at complete odds on this issue."

"Maybe." Morgan shook her head. "I don't know."

Stephen poked his head in. "Michael's coming around."

\* \* \* \* \*

His family was gathered around his bed when he opened his eyes and kept them open, looking from one person to the next. Libby, Morgan and Stephen stood aside, opposite from his mother as Michael gazed at her a long moment and then said her name. His mother collapsed against her younger son, Brian, who stood behind her, and then she squeezed Michael's hand and cried.

Michael closed his eyes a moment and mumbled, "Don't cry, Ma. I'll think I'm dying." And then to everyone's relief, he managed a small smile.

Dr. Rosenberg slid a penlight out of his pocket. "Okay wise guy. Look up here." He shined the light, checking for pupil reaction and had Michael follow his finger with his eyes. He instructed him to grasp his finger with each hand and squeeze. Then he had him roll one hand over the other, forward then backward.

"Do you know where you are?" the doctor asked him.

"A hospital, I assume. I was shot at. Two shots. One in the chest and I think the other hit my head." Michael lifted his arm to touch his head and saw the trail of wires. "Shit. *Am* I going to die?"

The doctor smiled grimly. "No, but you had us going for awhile." He cranked Michael's bed up as he spoke to his family. "I'll give you all ten minutes to visit, but then I'm going to insist he rest. This is a good sign, Michael, but you're not out of the woods yet. I'll be back to throw everybody out and then we'll talk."

Libby felt a surge of protectiveness in response to the doctor's words. She didn't know if Michael should be told just yet about the bullet in his head. But she wasn't family, so she had no say in the matter.

While his mother spoke to him, she waved their little group over from the corner and Libby's heart hammered wildly. Night after night she had stroked his chest and ran her lips along his jaw and kissed him, reveling in his warmth and feeling his nerves jump under her fingertips. But now she was afraid to go near him. While he slept, she had convinced herself that he needed her, and she gave herself over to him. He had looked so vulnerable and young. Throughout the night she would smooth out the worry lines along his forehead until his face relaxed and his full lips formed a soft curve. His thick lashes, fanning his cheekbones in sleep, made him appear almost boyish.

But this was no boy she was approaching. He looked very male—adult male. The sculpted muscle along his chest and the dark stubble of beard were testimony to the raw power and testosterone coursing through his body. He looked anything but vulnerable, and she was scared to death of his reaction to seeing her here. The last time they were together he had been furious with her and had stormed out of her apartment.

Stephen grabbed Michael's hand. "Hey, you've got a good grip for being comatose for days."

Michael's brow creased. "I've been out for days?"

Morgan jabbed Stephen in the shoulder. "Don't listen to him," she said to Michael. "It's good to see you awake. The doctor's right, though, you gave us quite a scare."

Libby wanted to throttle them both for their inept greetings but she hung back, torn between wanting to throw herself protectively around him or run out the door.

Michael peered around Morgan. "Libby?" His voice held a softness that made her heart ache.

"Yes, Michael. Hello." She smiled and reached out to take his hand.

He locked his hand around hers and held it and then impaled her with his eyes. Her own gaze skittered away a moment as she felt so many pairs of eyes focused on them. He pulled her subtly toward him. How could he be so strong after what he'd been through?

"You've been here," he said, more as a statement he sought to confirm.

She nodded.

"I felt you." He held her hand in a firm grip.

His mother spoke up but he kept his eyes on Libby. "Libby's been here throughout each night, Michael. The doctors say she was good for you."

"Is that right?" He lifted a brow at her.

"Your...your pulse," she stammered. "Dr. Rosenberg asked me to stay."

She watched his expression change, and he released his grip. Her moment of confusion disappeared when he spoke again. "I see." It was in his eyes as clear as if he voiced it. He thought she felt obligated. He nodded politely. "Thank you."

Her heart dropped to her feet. How could two people communicate so badly? If she weren't so surrounded by people, she would tell him now that she was in love with him. Or would she?

Moments later Dr. Rosenberg entered again and, true to his word, threw them all out. Michael barely glanced at her when she said goodnight.

# Chapter Fourteen

Libby didn't return the next day. She told Morgan she wanted to give him time with his family, but Morgan didn't believe it.

"You're running away," she accused Libby when she called from the hospital.

"I need some time to think."

"Like I said, you're running away."

"Has he asked for me?"

Other than an audible sigh, Morgan was silent.

"Well?"

"Libby, come and see him. Don't make him ask for you."

"Why not?" If Michael was so unsure about how he felt that he didn't ask for her then she couldn't go to him. She wanted all of him. For the first time things became clear. "If he wants me, Morgan, he knows where I am."

"Libby, the man's injured, in a weakened state."

"Does he look weak to you?"

Morgan sighed and Libby grew somber. "Morgan, the way I love him, if he asked me today to quit my job and stay home and raise his six kids I'm afraid I would do it. I would do anything for him and it scares me to death."

"Libby—"

"No, Morgan. If he asks for me, I'll go with my heart in my hand, but I won't chase him. I've surrendered enough of my dignity. I won't lose what little is left."

* * * * *

The next three weeks of her new job were a whirlwind of challenge and change since, to her surprise, she convinced her boss to try a new Internet program of sales. Working women, too busy to shop, could register their size and have clothes delivered and returned for a small monthly fee without ever having to enter a clothing department. The head of sales for Nordstrom's was skeptical, but her marketing department—usually the most innovative in any corporation—assured sales that any loss by quarter's end could be charged against marketing's budget.

Libby was grateful for the vote of confidence on her proposed project, but some days she lacked the energy to exhibit much enthusiasm. She had wondered if she suffered aftereffects from her miscarriage. Her doctor ran a battery of tests to reassure her.

She thought each day would get easier, but everyday she didn't hear from Michael was like rubbing a raw wound.

Morgan kept her apprised of his progress. After two weeks the hospital had released him and he had been given a full disability retirement from the Bureau. She learned he was relocating to North Jersey.

It took every ounce of willpower that Libby had to keep from thinking about him, and to make matters worse, her parents asked about him often, expressing confidence that she and Michael belonged together. She couldn't imagine how her parents could get that idea after seeing them together only once.

As if she weren't under enough stress, her father began pressuring her to "come over to the other side" since his corporate spies learned how well her new program was received by his competing executives and of the promising preliminary results of consumer focus groups.

He was offering her flex hours, more pay, and the option of telecommuting several days a week in favor of driving into an office five days. While months ago she would have been thrilled, the thought of another change left her exhausted.

As her workday wound down, Libby kicked off her heels and descended into the swivel chair behind her desk, too tired to do anything else. She studied the shimmery stockings she was testing out to see if their lacy elastic tops held firm throughout the busy day of a junior executive and she decided they had fared fine. This junior executive would choose them over pantyhose any morning.

She smoothed her linen skirt over the champagne silk stockings and remembered another time, a lifetime ago, when she had repeated the same nervous gesture under the piercing icy blue stare of a man who at first terrified her, and later fascinated her, and then had finally stolen her heart. Did he even know?

The phone startled her. As she reached for the receiver, she stuffed down any hope that it was he. Her doctor's concerned voice greeted her. The next few minutes were a blur of words and emotions as the doctor explained and apologized, sounding almost as shocked and befuddled as Libby felt. What the doctor was saying was impossible, and yet she assured Libby that it wasn't—certainly a rare occurrence but not impossible.

Libby replaced the receiver after she numbly made an appointment for the next day.

*Just when she thought things couldn't get any more complicated, they did.* With shaking hands she called Morgan.

A half hour later, completely overwhelmed and on the brink of despair over the events of the last three weeks and now the last mystifying hour, she laid her head on her desk and felt herself drift off to sleep. It was far easier than trying to figure out this impossibly complicated mess. At least now she had an excuse for her sleepiness.

She awoke sometime later to the feel of a large hand sifting through her hair. She sat up, startled, and looked into the deep blue of Michael's eyes. Her heart pounded in her chest at the wonderful sight of him.

He backed up and raised his hands aloft at her startled expression and went back around to the front of her desk, his smile tentative.

She rose slowly and came around to him, titling her face to look at him closely. She wanted to reach up and smooth back his hair, to stroke any new lines that had formed.

"Are you all right?"

"I've got a hole in my head." He gave her a small grin. "But then, you always thought I did."

She smiled at him, a reaction that seemed to surprise him.

He took a step forward and with the barest touch, laid his fingertips under her chin. His lips parted and he seemed on the verge of bending toward her, but then, as though thinking better of it, he backed up a step and ran a finger under his collar. It was all she could do to keep herself from leaning into him and begging him to hold her. After the turmoil of this afternoon it was everything she needed. But now, more than ever, she needed to know he was here for her and for no other reason.

"Did you talk to Morgan?" Libby didn't see how he could have. She glanced at the clock. She had hung up with her no more than an hour ago. And Morgan would never tell him anyway.

"Morgan?" His confusion was genuine.

Her mind worked overtime, but she coached herself in patience. When it came to talking, Michael could not be rushed. She should ask him to sit or offer him a drink, but she was reluctant to move and break this fragile connection. No man had ever made her feel so entirely female just by his presence.

*Oh, she was really losing her mind.*

But he moved away from her, restless. "No." He began pacing before her. "I need to talk to you," he said, running a quick hand through his hair.

She dropped slowly onto the couch and sat tense and still, perched on the edge. Locking her hands together in her lap, she held her breath.

He shoved his hands in his pockets and stopped before her, inhaling slowly and then finally letting out a long breath. "Thank you for staying with me at the hospital. The doctors explained what a critical difference it made."

She stifled a sigh of disappointment. He was here to thank her.

He bent his head and then looked back up at her. "And..." his eyes glinted in amusement, "the nurses offered to continue the treatment you gave me at night."

*She could just imagine.* Her cheeks burned. It was embarrassing that they had seen her but then to describe to him how she had stroked his muscles and kissed his neck endlessly? She dropped her gaze and studied her nails.

"But that's not what I came to say. I need to tell you that I was on my way to figuring it out." When she looked up, he was kneading the back of his neck and directing his words to the carpet as he paced.

"I made some phone calls while I was recuperating in the hospital." He glanced at her. "I would have come sooner but the week I was released my brother needed me in court. Another custody hearing—"

"Michael." She jumped up. "As soon as you got out of the hospital?" she asked incredulously, picturing him dragging his way to New York for his brother while he was supposed to be resting. "Who's taking care of *you*?" She stepped closer.

He blinked in surprise and stopped his pacing. "No one...I'm fine." His eyes grew soft and then he slid his hand up her neck.

She wanted to lean into his touch. It would be so easy and the thought made her grow warm, but at this significant moment it would only make things more complicated.

"Why are you here, Michael?" she asked softly.

He settled his hand on her shoulder. "That's what I'm trying to say. I found a way to settle our differences, but I didn't want to tell you until I had it all worked out."

"You mean you figured this out when you thought I was still pregnant?"

"No. On the day I got shot. It was the day I found out you had resigned." He cupped her face with both hands. "I was walking and decided I'd take a job teaching science like I had always wanted. Coach football, too. I've had enough offers over the years but never considered it with the high cost of supporting a family."

She cautioned herself, tempering her hopes. "Why are you telling me this, Michael?"

He grabbed her hands and pressed them to his lips. "Because I can't lose you, Libby. And I'm willing to make compromises to win you." He drew her over to the couch and sat her down. "It's no use fighting it. The first day I saw you I felt like an electric jolt hit me, but I told myself I wasn't interested. When I learned how important you considered your career, I *convinced* myself I wasn't interested. And then when I heard you were from the Upper East Side..." He gave a low chuckle. "I told myself I'd be crazy to get involved with you."

He reached up and with gentle fingers stroked along her jawline. "Then I was stupid enough to think I could make love to you and be done with it. I guess that's the night I fell in love with you." His voice was a low whisper. He traced her lower lip with his thumb. "We're like Newton's third law. For every force there's an equal and opposite one. That's us."

She didn't know whether to laugh or cry. But she was too filled with emotion to speak.

"Libby? Should I be worried that you're not saying anything?"

All the anxiety of the day, the month, came rushing forward and burst through her in choking sobs. He drew her onto his lap and held her, stroking her with strong, sure caresses and murmuring nonsensical reassurances that nonetheless reassured her.

"There's a Nordstrom's," he continued, murmuring into her hair, "up in North Jersey where I got a job." He ran his lips along her forehead. "I'm not saying you have to transfer. I could look around here. It's just a suggestion."

"You would do that?" She sat up and looked at him.

He nodded and threaded his fingers through her hair. "Hell, with my disability retirement, I could get by without working at all for awhile, but a 'house husband'? I think that's pushing it." He frowned at her.

She burst into soft laughter. "I don't know," she teased. "The thought of you greeting me in Saran Wrap has possibilities."

"Very funny." He scowled and drew her against him, settling her into the crook of his arm. "Is it a deal?"

"Ask me, Michael." For all her belief in equality, she wanted him to propose. And being the Neanderthal that he was, he knew it.

He slid her off his lap and dropped down on one knee before her. Taking her hand in his, his gaze intense and studying her, he said, "I love you, Libby. Will you marry me?"

She stroked the rough shadow of his beard. "I love you, Michael Mulcahy. Yes, I'll marry you."

As the tears streamed down her face, he kissed each one away. "We don't have to have kids right away, either. I know it's important for you to get settled in your career."

"It's a little late for that."

He stopped kissing her, his eyes questioning. Then a pain swept across his gaze. "If there's a problem since your miscarriage, we'll work it out. We can make this work, Libby." He held her face between his hands, his eyes asking her to agree. "Libby?"

She smiled. "My father's offered me very flexible hours and work at home." She covered his hands. "I think, under the circumstances, I should take him up on it."

"What circumstances?"

"Apparently, your sperm isn't as ineffective as we thought and I'm pretty fertile, too."

"What do you mean?"

"I expelled the incomplete fertilization but I'm still pregnant."

His eyes widened. "You're still carrying my baby?"

"Not exactly." What was such a shock an hour ago now filled her with happiness. She pressed her lips gently to his. "I'm carrying two of your babies."

"Two?" His mouth dropped and then he made a choking sound. He grabbed onto her shoulders. "Are you sure? How is that possible?"

"My words exactly. But the sonogram technician reported two healthy fetuses to my doctor. It wasn't what she had been looking for when she ordered the test but there they were."

He lifted himself slowly and sank down onto the couch beside her, staring ahead, stunned.

And then, to her surprise, he laughed, a deep rich laughter that set her pulse racing.

He pulled her close and nuzzled her neck. "Jesus, I'm happy, Libby."

"Me too." She sighed. "You're wonderful, Michael," she murmured, rubbing her nose playfully with his. "You're not a Neanderthal at all."

"Oh, yes I am." He lifted her easily, settling her onto his lap. "Let's celebrate." He began popping the buttons on her blouse.

"Michael." She clutched her blouse closed. "It's only four o'clock, the floor is teeming with people."

"Send your secretary home." He pushed aside her hand and ran his tongue along her cleavage. She felt him harden beneath her. Desire flooded her, followed by sheer panic. She squirmed off his lap.

He walked swiftly to the door. "What's her name?"

"Who?"

"Your secretary."

"It's a him…Kevin. Michael—"

He swung the door open. "You can leave, Kevin. Ms. Vandermark won't need you for the rest of the day." He slammed the door and locked it.

"Michael." She smiled. "This isn't the Bureau. I barely know these people."

"Libby…" His face darkened. "It seems like forever since I've been inside you and I'm not waiting another second."

His words brought a new flood of arousal to soak her panties. "Michael, it's just that—"

"It's time you learned who's in charge." His voice dropped a pitch. "Now strip off that blouse. Real slow."

"Michael," she laughed. "I take it back. You *are* a Neanderthal. Now come on…"

As he walked toward her, his pace slow and deliberate, he said silkily, "I'm more of an australopithecine but I'm not going to dicker over anthropology. I'm more interested in biology." His gaze swept lewdly over her breasts. Her nipples hardened deliciously. A small smile lit the corner of his lips.

A gentle knock on the door sounded. "Libby, you okay?"

"Go away," Michael growled over his shoulder.

"It's all right, Kevin, you can go. See you tomorrow."

"Michael…" She fumbled to close the open buttons of her blouse as she slowly backed away. "Anyone could come—" She bumped into her desk, reaching her hand back to steady herself.

"Are you disobeying me, Libby?" His eyes glittered and he kept coming. Her mouth gaped.

He unbuckled his belt with slow considering movements and boldly locked his eyes onto hers. "Don't *make* me turn you over my knee."

"Michael," she choked. "You wouldn't dare—"

He released a throaty chuckle. "Oh, wouldn't I." Then he held the belt in one large hand and flexed the other.

"Oh…" Her gazed dropped involuntarily to his hand, and she was suddenly breathless with the image of being turned over his hard thighs, her bottom bared to his wicked gaze, and she became embarrassingly aroused at the thought. She was *really* losing her mind. His erection strained against his Levis, the faded soft fabric outlining far more than was decent.

He dropped the belt and ripped his T-shirt up over his head before descending onto the couch. "I'm waiting." He kicked off his shoes, his eyes filled with male intent as he perched on the edge and followed her every move.

With calculated slowness, she threaded each button from its hole. He leaned forward, his gaze riveted on her nipples, hard and thrusting against the flimsy material of her blouse. A rosy flush spread through her just watching his arousal heighten further as she drew aside the silky fabric to reveal the satin uplift bra that only half covered her nipples. A heavy pulse throbbed at the base of his neck. "Like Hershey kisses," he murmured, his eyes glazed with lust. "Keep going," he rasped, his jaw flexing with tension.

She unzipped her skirt and let it fall, anticipating his reaction to the lacy stockings.

"Jesus, Libby." He winced and unzipped his fly. Her breath caught as he shoved down his jeans and threw them off without a trace of self-consciousness and sat before her, fully erect and watching her. "Don't stop now," he said, his voice thready with arousal. Stop? She wanted to faint. "Unhook your bra."

She moaned inwardly, her insides shaking, but with her struggle for confidence came a pleasing realization. The realization of her power over him. She smiled to herself. "You promise not to spank me?"

She watched as his thick cock jerked in response to her words. He closed his eyes and moaned before dropping awkwardly to his knees and crawling toward her, his erection reducing him to a slow painful pace. "That's right, Mulcahy, on your knees," she chuckled. When he reached her, he grabbed her hips and licked her navel. She stifled a groan.

"Don't think just because you have me crawling and begging, that you've won, Libby."

His hands skimmed along her stockings where they met her skin and then he leaned back on his heels and watched himself stroke the V between her legs with his thumbs. She drew a sharp breath and her legs gave way.

In record speed he stretched her out along the carpet, stripping off her panties in one smooth movement. "We'll leave the stockings on," he groaned.

He lowered his weight, pinning her to the carpet, and licked along her jaw. "I've got you now." He throbbed against her. "Who's in charge, Libby?" he murmured into her neck, drawing her delicate skin between his teeth.

"Michael...I'm burning up." She spread herself, drawing up her knees, begging him to take her. "Stop teasing me."

"Who's teasing?" He smiled against her lips and then licked in fluttery strokes to torment her. She sought his tongue, reaching for him wildly, but he arched his neck just enough to hold her at bay.

"Michael."

"Who's master, Libby?" He threaded his fingers through her hair and made her look at him.

"Michael, I'm going to kill you."

Deep laughter vibrated through him. "You won't have the energy, I guarantee you."

He thrust her arms over her head, hovering over her nipples, his breath hot and tantalizing, licking with the gentlest of touches.

"Give up?" he teased her.

A shuddering need overwhelmed her, the gentle torture too exquisite. "I need you, Michael," she breathed.

He groaned and buried his lips in her neck. "Good enough," he growled and slid his lips along her stomach and buried his mouth between her legs.

"No," she breathed. "I can't take it. I need you inside me."

He ignored her and spread her sex with his fingers and licked. She screamed out and arched into his tongue, the heat and tension bringing her to a fevered pitch. She was ready to explode. He stopped and then barely flicked her tiny bud with the tip of his tongue. She cried out her frustration. Then he crawled back up her body and spread her legs wide. He slid into her, inch by punishing inch. The feel of him filling her was more than sexual fulfillment; it was a completion. And her love for him soared.

Then he stopped midway. "Are you sure we can fuck?" A sweat broke over his broad back.

"Michael," she gasped. "I'm going to kill you." She thrashed under him.

"I'll go slow and easy," he promised, his voice raw. He shifted inside her, rock-hard now.

He drew a soft moan from her that quickly turned to a tortured whimper when he stilled. "What are you doing?"

He touched his lips to her brow in a caress so tender she wanted to throttle him.

"Michael!"

"I don't want to hurt the babies." He slipped out again, agonizingly slow.

"Don't you dare." She struggled to feel him deeper. He entered her again but this time with careful, measured strokes that kept her burning and bereft, reaching for something he wouldn't give her.

He ran his lips along her forehead and down her cheek. "I love you, Libby." He kissed her gently.

She bit him…so hard that she drew blood and a roar of surprise from him. "Take me," she sobbed.

With a guttural growl he thrust into her, hard and deep. Then his mouth was on hers, demanding. The taste of blood on his tongue added to the erotic charge.

She scratched at his back and gave herself over to him and to the blissful heat and pleasure, knowing he would protect her as she met his bold thrusts. Then she drew up tight and came apart, drowning in a pool of pure delight, her entire body burning up in a wave of sheer sexual heat.

He shuddered with the feel of her drawing him into her body. He tensed and stopped breathing. And then with one hard thrust she felt his release finally thunder through him. She held him close.

He collapsed against her. "It'll take more than a lifetime to get enough of you."

"I'm counting on that." She smiled against his neck, content to lie there forever. "I love you, Michael."

He raised himself on his elbows and traced his lips along her hairline. When he looked at her, his gaze was somber. "I'll always love you."

"Promise?"

He nodded gravely and pressed his lips to hers.

"Even if I ask you to come to the ballet with me this weekend?"

His lips stopped. "Ballet?"

"Yes. My mother can get an extra ticket." She smiled dreamily at him when he drew back to face her.

"You want *me* to go?"

"Of course."

He looked thoughtful a moment and then he smiled. "Okay...and then on Sunday we can go to the Jets game." He nipped at her lips.

"The Jets?" she asked incredulously, pulling away from his kisses to talk to him. "You mean, as in football?"

"Sure."

"I have a better idea." She reached up to draw his lips closer. "How about if you go to the game with my father and I'll go to the ballet with my mother—"

"And then," he finished, "we can come home and make love all night."

"Mmm...now that's a plan."

*Enjoy this excerpt from*

# A MAN'S DESIRE

*© Copyright Kathryn Ann Dubois 2003*

# Chapter One
*New Orleans, 1798*

Ethan Peron never squandered his pleasures.

The conviction rose from childhood poverty and a cynical adult's certainty of the shifting fortunes of men. Over the years he had developed an order, a precise routine in the manner in which he savored his sensual delights, a routine from which he rarely wavered and which bespoke admirable control.

Drink first. Whiskey mostly, sometimes brandy, which he swirled lazily in a heated crystal snifter as he did tonight, allowing the mesmerizing twirl of the glossy amber liquid to relax his mind and clear it of the week's business. One smooth sip coated his throat and burned a path straight to his gut. He sighed in satisfaction. Even the etched cut of the glass intrigued him tonight. With the tip of one calloused finger, he traced the vine of gold relief that trailed along its stem, feeling himself unwind with the idle gesture.

This evening, as always, he would take considerable time pondering his second pleasure. As he cast a lazy glance over the club's offerings, he remained free from annoying flirtations and open invitations. His habits included drinking alone, in the silence of his thoughts.

It was well understood.

When the occasional ambitious woman who harbored hopes of attaining mistress status disturbed his routine, a swift dismissal followed. Madame Thibault tolerated no rebelliousness from her girls and prided her establishment on its sensitivity to the eccentricities of its male patrons, particularly Ethan, given the Madame's and his fond history.

Too often of late his thoughts returned to that history and his youthful initiation into the treasures of women. And like an old man recounting more exciting times, he relived now his innocent surprise at seeing naked female flesh within touching distance for the first time.

So suddenly had he halted that day in the brothel hallway, twenty-two years ago, that the lid of the chamber pot he held as he performed his morning rounds slid dangerously to one side while he stood in the open doorway of Lizelle's room and gaped.

Even now Ethan smiled, recalling how he looked—a tall lanky youth, dark of hair and eyes, but soft of face. Too pretty, Madame Thibault claimed, to be considered a man despite the adult urgency with which his boy's body had reacted. A tinge of pride still lingered.

His innocent eyes had roved over Lizelle's smooth bottom as she bent to slide her toes into her stocking. Ethan, momentarily ignoring the pot he clutched, tilted his head to one side and bent low and then lower, hoping to glimpse heaven in the sweet pink lips he had studied only in discarded magazines, their forbidden pages stained and crumpled, leaving more to imagination than actual sight.

She bent lower and he swooned. The fleshy folds pouted through her silken thighs, even her tiny brown rose between the smooth globes of her bottom winked at him. His every impulse cried to drop to his knees and lick her. He grew painfully erect.

"What is dis?" Madame Thibault's smooth voice sounded behind him.

He whirled in a panic and stared wide-eyed as his employer approached in a swirl of red silk, her dark hair pinned up hastily with two clips and her ample breasts swaying freely under the form shaping fabric. She'd just emerged from her bath. He could smell the tang of rose water on her moist skin.

Sure he would be fired for being caught ogling the merchandise, he muttered a quick apology. "I didn't know Lizelle was still in her room." He gave a quick bow of deference and waited.

Lizelle's throaty chuckle sounded behind him, and then he felt her warm breath brush the back of his neck.

"What luck, *non*?" She ran a long nail along the side of his throat. He dared not turn to look at her but he could smell her, too. More woman scent to tease his senses.

Madame Thibault eyed him with interest. "You value your job, *Mon chéri*?"

"Yes, Madame."

"'Dis mus' be hard for you," she murmured, "surrounded by so much female flesh and sounds of couplin' behind every door, *non*?"

"No, Madame."

"*Non*?" She arched a brow and dropped her eyes to his rigid erection. His face burned but still he grew harder.

Her nipples pouted beneath the silky fabric of her dressing gown and it gaped wide, exposing a creamy expanse of cleavage. He had never seen a woman's nipples — girls' but never the fully ripened peaks of a woman.

The temptation to touch his finger to her nipple goaded his reckless nature. But before he did, she cupped his sex and squeezed. The rush of blood to his face sent his head spinning. When she scratched her long nails over the soft cloth of his breeches, he held his breath.

"He's a fine lookin' young man, our Ethan. Is he *non*, Lizelle?"

"Oh, *oui*, Madame."

"And he's a fine age. Just the right age. Don' you agree?"

"*Oui*, Madame. May I?"

"*Mais, non…*" Madame laughed softly, trailing her fingertips along his length before finally releasing him. He gave a sigh of relief. But then she cupped his cheek and smiled with a warm drawing smile that held delightful promise. "I have so few pleasures left. 'Dis one is mine."

She took his hand and led him to the bedchamber that overlooked downtown New Orleans and boasted the largest balcony in the city. Ethan disbelieved that he stood in the Madame's private chamber. As she led him to a plush velvet chair in the room's center, his eyes roved over the gilded framed paintings that graced the brocade walls.

One oil portrayed a flaxen haired woman, reclining on plump pillows with one man bracing her from behind, palms lifting her breasts, while another's face buried between her legs. A hot rush of desire pumped through Ethan, threatening to explode over into his breeches.

"You like my paintings," the Madame breathed silkily, a knowing smile tilting the corners of her lush mouth.

Ethan couldn't think for the blood rushing to his groin. If she touched him now, he would go off.

She eased him into the chair and stood before him, her plump tits outlined perfectly under the smooth silk of her robe. When he licked his lips in an unconscious gesture, she gave a husky chuckle that caused a blush to rise up his neck.

"*Mon chéri.*" She smiled tenderly. "Be not embarrassed by your manly desires." She caressed his cheek and moved closer, her woman scent filling him, sparking a new charge of arousal.

He gazed at her with adoring eyes. "Madame, pardon, but I don't know what to do."

"Jus' do what comes natural," she crooned, brushing her breasts across his face in encouragement. Her open invitation erased any lingering reluctance.

Without further hesitation, he slid both hands into her robe until he covered her smooth mounds and then he stroked, groaning with pleasure at the feel of her tits pebbling under his palms. Anxious to see her, he slipped the robe off her shoulders, letting it fall to her waist and looked his fill. He sucked in a breath at the sight of large brown nipples that seemed to beg for his tongue. He captured a nipple between his lips, the velvet feel of it on his tongue hinting of heaven. Her startled gasp when he suckled her hard emboldened him.

"You are mos' skillful, my boy," she murmured, threading her fingers through his thick ebony hair as she cradled him to her breast and guided him to the other. When he flicked his tongue over the tender tips, she shuddered.

He wanted to feel her everywhere.

In an eager rush, he unbelted her robe, pushing the cool silk off her rounded hips to pool at her ankles, his heart hammering at the thought of seeing her most private of places. His heart stopped at the sight of her smooth belly and thighs surrounding the downy mound.

He filled with seed, the throbbing of his cock now precariously out of control. He closed his eyes against the thought of her pink fleshy lips hidden behind her curls. He let out a low moan.

The scent of her sex drew his eyes open. She had stepped closer. Unable to resist, he licked her. The moment his tongue touched the hot supple flesh between her legs, he exploded in hot spurts, his come pumping through him in thundering jets. He grabbed onto her thighs and groaned, burying his face in her soft belly, mortified by his ineptness.

But she just brushed his hair off his forehead and spoke to him in a soothing tone. "Now that we've taken the edge off, *Mon chéri*, we can enjoy ourselves."

With those reassuring words, she stepped over to the bed and stretched herself out across its large expanse, still naked and spreading herself for him, motioning to his fully clothed body. As he tore off his shirt and worked the laces of his soaked breeches, his eyes fixed on her long painted nail stroking between her thighs. Her lips swelled to a deep red, and she moaned as she raked her nails along the plump layers.

He wanted to see her, examine every inch of her. By the time he flung off his shoes and breeches, he was hard again from imagining the feel of sinking into her silky depths.

She spread her legs wider. In rapture he watched her slide one long tapered finger between the plush glistening lips. It disappeared.

"I want to do that," he choked.

She slid her finger out and licked it.

He groaned and dove between her legs, slipping his tongue between the soft folds and exploring her ripe lips with his fingers and tasting. Her sweetness promised heaven and the tiny gasps and sighs she released with each lick fired his blood. He wanted to devour her.

When a tiny pearl swelled at the top of her lips, he suckled it greedily. She arched her hips and cried out.

"I'm sorry, Madame." He jumped up and sat back on his heels, his shaft jutting out from his stomach like a flagpole.

But she spread her treasures with two fingers and revealed all of the pearl. "'Dis is the center of my pleasure, young Ethan."

He stared hungrily at the dewy jewel.

"I'll teach you 'bout women and I will die from the pleasure of it," she said on a sigh and writhed under his hot gaze. "Such an eager boy. I have much to share."

\* \* \* \* \*

Ethan smiled to himself now, remembering the years of lessons under her patient tutorage and remembering the first feel of her hot soft depths as he sank to the hilt. Never had he imagined such bliss and nothing since had compared to that first time of wonder.

In his youthful exuberance he had pledged his undying love to the lusty Madame, to which she had chuckled in delight.

Often, in the years that followed, he expressed his love for her, but now it embodied the mature love of two friends who had experienced much of life. She remained one of the few people he trusted.

He smiled at her fondly now. Though the years had angled the once soft contours of her face, and her black hair had lost some of its rich luster, her beauty still endured for a woman her age, any age.

"Ethan, darling, how was your week?" she asked in the educated speech of a shrewd businesswoman, the Cajun French of her youth a memory.

"The same," he said, lifting her hand to his lips. "And you?"

"No surprises," she responded, sinking gracefully into the chair beside him. With a subtle motion of her chin, a young dark-haired beauty slipped a shimmering goblet into Madame Thibault's hand.

Before the girl could retreat, Madame circled her wrist and turned her to Ethan. "This is Paulette." She smiled. "She's new."

"And very young." Ethan raised a brow.

"As you were once, *Mon chéri*." Marie Thibault laughed. "She needs a gentle hand, Ethan."

The girl licked her lips, her eyes darting about as they spoke.

Taking girls held no rank in his list of pleasures and his friend well knew it, but as always, she would try.

"I was thinking along the lines of Monique tonight," he answered. The redhead had a penchant for spanking, and he liked the feel of her lush curves, warm under his palms.

"I see." She sighed in disappointment, and then with a flick of her hand sent the young girl away. "It's no use trying to convince you. You're very definite in your pleasures."

He nodded and took a soothing sip of his brandy, holding it on his tongue for a beat and then letting it trickle along the edges of his throat. After he finished his drink he would spank and fuck Monique, tip his hand at high stakes poker, and savor a Cuban cigar, all in that order, and leave a satisfied man.

For Ethan never squandered his pleasures. Drink, women, cards, and cigars. In that order. He never wavered.

Ethan Peron…was bored.

## About the author:

Kathryn Anne Dubois lives the demanding life of a mother of five, a wife of 30+ years, and a public school art teacher. What better reason to escape into the delicious fantasy world of writing romantica. Reviewer Lani Roberts of Affair de Coeur Magazine has this to say of Kathryn. "Kathryn Anne Dubois makes her debut...with such sexual intensity that the readers will definitely cry for more." Kathryn was first published in 1999 with Virgin Publishing's Black Lace Line whose publisher's claim "only the most arousing fiction makes it into a Black Lace - erotica at the cutting edge written by women for women", and later with Red Sage's Secrets. She still writes for both publications. She is pleased to have joined the wonderful authors of Ellora's Cave. Kathryn has been an active member of Romance Writers of America since 1998 and lives in the greater Philadelphia area.

Kathryn Anne Dubois welcomes mail from readers. You can write to her c/o Ellora's Cave Publishing at 1337 Commerce Drive, Suite 13, Stow OH 44224.

# Why an electronic book?

We live in the Information Age—an exciting time in the history of human civilization in which technology rules supreme and continues to progress in leaps and bounds every minute of every hour of every day. For a multitude of reasons, more and more avid literary fans are opting to purchase e-books instead of paperbacks. The question to those not yet initiated to the world of electronic reading is simply: *why?*

1. *Price.* An electronic title at Ellora's Cave Publishing runs anywhere from 40-75% less than the cover price of the <u>exact same title</u> in paperback format. Why? Cold mathematics. It is less expensive to publish an e-book than it is to publish a paperback, so the savings are passed along to the consumer.

2. *Space.* Running out of room to house your paperback books? That is one worry you will never have with electronic novels. For a low one-time cost, you can purchase a handheld computer designed specifically for e-reading purposes. Many e-readers are larger than the average handheld, giving you plenty of screen room. Better yet, hundreds of titles can be stored within your new library—a single microchip. (Please note that Ellora's Cave does not endorse any specific brands. You can check our website at www.ellorascave.com

for customer recommendations we make available to new consumers.)

3. *Mobility.* Because your new library now consists of only a microchip, your entire cache of books can be taken with you wherever you go.

4. *Personal preferences are accounted for.* Are the words you are currently reading too small? Too large? Too...**ANNOYING**? Paperback books cannot be modified according to personal preferences, but e-books can.

5. *Innovation.* The way you read a book is not the only advancement the Information Age has gifted the literary community with. There is also the factor of what you can read. Ellora's Cave Publishing will be introducing a new line of interactive titles that are available in e-book format only.

6. *Instant gratification.* Is it the middle of the night and all the bookstores are closed? Are you tired of waiting days—sometimes weeks—for online and offline bookstores to ship the novels you bought? Ellora's Cave Publishing sells instantaneous downloads 24 hours a day, 7 days a week, 365 days a year. Our e-book delivery system is 100% automated, meaning your order is filled as soon as you pay for it.

Those are a few of the top reasons why electronic novels are displacing paperbacks for many an avid reader. As always, Ellora's Cave Publishing welcomes your questions and comments. We invite you to email us at service@ellorascave.com or write to us directly at: 1337 Commerce Drive, Suite 13, Stow OH 44224.

Discover for yourself why readers can't get enough of the multiple award-winning publisher Ellora's Cave. Whether you prefer e-books or paperbacks, be sure to visit EC on the web at www.ellorascave.com for an erotic reading experience that will leave you breathless.

Printed in the United States
30818LVS00009B/130-156

9 781419 950094